Stringybark Summer

by

JUDITH O'NEILL

Hamish Hamilton · London

By the same author

Jess and the River Kids

First published in Great Britain 1985 by
Hamish Hamilton Children's Books
Garden House, 57 – 59 Long Acre, London WC2E 9JZ

British Library Cataloguing in Publication Data
O'Neill, Judith
Stringybark Summer.
I. Title
823 [J] PZ7
ISBN 0-241-11698-8

Typeset by VAP Group Limited
Kidlington, Oxfordshire
Printed in Great Britain by
The Thetford Press Ltd
Thetford, Norfolk

For John
and Rachel, Catherine and Philippa

Contents

Eighty years ago there was a sawmill like Stringybark Mill in the Otway Forest, Victoria, Australia, but all the characters and events in this story are imaginary.

1. *Goodbye to the Farm*

Sophie woke early to the familiar Monday-morning sound of her mother splitting firewood. She sat up in bed and pulled back the dark curtain to let the summer light flood into her room on the far corner of the back verandah. Even at six o'clock in the morning the sunshine was white hot. Today was going to be another scorcher, just like yesterday and the day before that. Shielding her eyes from the glare with her hands, Sophie looked out into the back yard. There was her mother, bending over the chopping block just outside the wash-house door. One hand grasped a long-handled axe near its head. The other hand held a thick log upright on the block. With a few sharp jabbing strokes of the axe, her mother split off one rough chunk of wood after another. They clattered to the ground around the block and lay there, higgledy-piggledy, in the early morning sunlight.

As Sophie watched, her mother slowly straightened herself and stood upright again. Her brown hessian apron was strained tight around her bulging figure. Only five weeks now until the new baby was supposed to come. Sophie felt a sudden spurt of anger that her mother should still be having to chop firewood at this late stage. It wasn't right. She jumped out of bed, found her grey flannel dressing-gown, and shuffled along the verandah in her slippers. Her brown hair was still screwed up tight into an untidy halo of rag ringlets. Muffin, the black cat, was waiting for her by the steps and mewing loudly for food.

"Wait on, Muff," muttered Sophie, running across the yard to the wash-house. "I've got to give Mother a hand first."

Muffin followed her, still mewing.

"Mother!" shouted Sophie. "You shouldn't be chopping wood! It's ridiculous! Let me do it! Where's Dad?"

"In bed of course," said her mother in a matter-of-fact voice, pushing a strand of greying hair back behind her ear. "You can't do it, Sophie. You'd only hurt yourself."

"I've got to learn some time, haven't I? Give me a try. Go on."

Mother handed over the axe. Sophie lifted up a new log, standing it endways on the block as she'd seen her mother do on a hundred Monday mornings.

"Do be careful now, Sophie. I'll just get the fire going." And Mother gathered up an armful of the split firewood, stooping awkwardly to reach the scattered pieces, and carried them into the wash-house.

Sophie let her axe fall heavily onto the log but it bounced off again at once, barely scratching the surface. She changed her grip on the handle and brought down the axe a second time. She used more force but with no better success.

"Cut along the grain," her mother called from the wash-house door.

Sophie looked for the grain in the wood and found it. She turned the log. She lifted her axe again. This time it bit into the wood—an inch at least. It was wedged in so tightly that she couldn't pull it out again. She lifted it slowly, log and all, and swung it heavily downwards. As the log hit the chopping-block, one crooked splintery sliver of wood broke off and fell at her feet.

"I can do it, Mother! I can do it!" shouted Sophie triumphantly.

Her mother came out to watch. Sophie still handled the axe stiffly but she was getting the knack and soon a shower of firewood was tumbling to the ground.

"Put your legs further apart. That makes it easier. Here, you need my boots. It's dangerous in those thin slippers."

Mother pulled off her black boots and Sophie pulled them on. She took up another tough log, planted her two feet well apart and tackled the smooth grainy surface of the wood with her axe. She was working more quickly now but her arms ached, her back ached and even her legs ached.

"How do you put up with this, Mother? Every single Monday! Doesn't it hurt your back?" Sophie panted out her words between the quick strokes of her axe.

"I've got used to it. The wash has to be done."

"Why won't Dad chop the wood? This is his axe after all."

"He's got the farm. He's busy enough. Chopping wood is a woman's work."

Sophie grunted as another log split.

"That'll soon be enough," said her mother. "Just finish off

that log and you can put the axe away."

When the log was done, Sophie carried her last load into the wash-house. Already a good fire was roaring away under the copper. The water was warming up. Two deep troughs stood ready for the rinse — one filled with clear cold water and the other with blue. A huge high wringer straddled the space between them. Sophie pulled off the heavy boots.

Mother took up a slab of her own home-made yellow soap and cut off paper-thin shavings with an old knife. They fell into the copper and floated around on the moving water. She pushed in the sheets, the white towels, the shirts, the thin cotton singlets, the grubby handkerchiefs. She poked and stirred the tumbling brew with a long wooden stick. The water began to boil at the edges and she clapped a round wooden lid on to the copper. She bent slowly to push two more bits of wood into the blazing fire. The whole wash-house was full of the pleasant smells of burning wood and hot soapy water.

"Let's get the breakfast ready, Sophie," said Mother, pushing her feet back into the boots. "We can leave all this now. You've got to be off by nine, remember."

Sophie remembered. She clung on tightly to her mother's arm as they walked across the back yard, up the steps and along the verandah, Muffin still trotting hopefully behind them or darting right under their feet.

"Mother, why do I have to go? You need me here. There's lots I could do to help you. And when the baby comes . . ." Sophie's voice trailed off. She wasn't sure what it would really be like when the baby came after Christmas.

Her mother sighed wearily.

"Let's not go over all that again, Sophie. I know you don't want to go but you're going all the same. Having a baby at my age is no easy matter. Mrs Flack will be here to see me through and I'd only be worried to have you hanging around the house, hearing things you shouldn't hear. It's no place for a girl of twelve. I want you out of the way just now."

"Mother!" protested Sophie. "You treat me like a child!"

"You *are* a child. Whatever made you think you weren't? Now set this table quickly and then get dressed. I can hear your father on the move. He'll be down in a minute."

When Sophie came back into the kitchen wearing her best brown dress for travelling, her black stockings and her solid lace-up shoes, all the white rags were out of her hair and the fat cork-screw curls were tied neatly back with a brown ribbon. Her father was already at his breakfast. He was eating thick slices of cold roast mutton with a shining golden pickled onion and a slab of brown bread and butter. He sat squarely, both elbows propped on the kitchen table. He ate slowly and steadily without a word to anyone. Sophie came and sat beside him but he didn't look up. She smoothed down her white lace collar.

"Are you taking Sophie, Tom, or is Charlie going to do it?" Mother threw the question over her shoulder from the black fire stove where she stood making the tea, her back towards Dad. Slowly and reluctantly Dad lifted his eyes from his plate of mutton and looked at Sophie with a puzzled frown.

"Sophie?" he mumbled, his mouth full of meat. "Where's Sophie off to now?"

Mother swung round, the teapot in her hand.

"Tom, you know very well she's going down to Dot's today. We talked it all over weeks ago. You agreed to the whole thing. Don't tell me you've forgotten already!"

"Dot's?" Dad sounded suspicious. "And how's she going to get the whole way down there?"

"In the train, of course. How else could she get there?" Mother's voice had a note of tired exasperation. "It leaves Birregurra at half past ten so she'll have to be away from here at nine. That just gives her time for a cup of tea with Mrs Dunphy before the train goes."

"And who's taking her into Birregurra?" asked Dad grumpily as if he already feared the worst.

"That's just what I was asking you. Are you taking her or is it Charlie?"

"I can't spare Charlie. You know that. He's only just finished the milking. Then there's the fencing to be done this morning. I'll have to take her myself, I suppose, but it couldn't have come on a worse day."

"What's wrong with the day, Dad?" asked Sophie timidly.

"I've got too much work to do, girl. That's what's wrong with it. Today and every day. Your mother makes all these plans of hers and then forgets to tell me. I've got to work on the dam in the bottom paddock today. It's in a mess."

"I did tell you, Tom. You've just forgotten," said Mother sharply. "Sophie will be ready at the front gate at nine."

Dad ate the rest of his meal in silence, now and then gazing out of the open window and across the parched home paddock with half-closed eyes. Cows were drifting away slowly from the milking-shed and bunching together in the thin shade of a clump of wattles. Sophie and her mother exchanged a glance over his head.

"You'd better finish your packing, Sophie," said Mother. "And don't forget those white pinnies and the hair-rags. I've got a couple of things for Auntie Dot and my letter to Grandpa. It'll get there quicker this week if you take it. Have you fed Muffin?"

Sophie shook her head.

"Well, just give her some milk. I've got no scraps today. She can find mice enough in the barn at this time of year."

Out on the back steps, Sophie poured the creamy milk into Muffin's blue saucer.

"Goodbye Muffin," she said, stroking the warm black fur. "I wish I didn't have to go." Muffin went on lapping quietly and intently at the milk.

By nine o'clock Sophie was standing outside the front gate, her yellow straw hat tied under her chin and the brim turned up. The bundle of clothes, rolled in a crocheted blanket and well roped together, lay on the ground beside her. Round behind the homestead Mother's first wash was already flapping on a long clothes-line that stretched from barn to milking-shed. A wooden prop gripped the line at its half-way point and lifted the wet washing high up into the wind. Mother came round the side of the house now, drying her red hands on the hessian apron.

"Sophie, did you remember to tell Miss Edgar that you wouldn't be back at school this year?"

Sophie gave a glum nod.

"What did she say?"

"She said it didn't matter. She told me to read some books over Christmas. She gave me a list."

"Books! You won't find many books down there at Auntie Dot's!"

Sophie shrugged her shoulders.

"I don't care," she said.

"Anyway, you won't have time for reading. Auntie Dot'll have plenty for you to do. Mind you do what she tells you now. And keep well away from those horses. You know what your father thinks about them."

Sophie nodded again. She stared up into the huge oak tree that had been growing there by the front gate of the homestead for more than fifty years. Dad's father had planted two of them when he'd first cleared the land and fenced it in. One had died in a bad drought, way back in those early days, but the other had put down good strong roots. It had flourished there by the front gate quite as well as any native gum tree and Sophie had spent many a summer's day up in the branches of her grandfather's oak. She had a favourite seat there on a broad smooth branch with the wide trunk for a back-rest and a screen of leaves for shade. Mother didn't seem to mind the long hours she perched up in her tree reading book after book, and Dad never even noticed she was there at all. He'd often walked right underneath her hiding place but he'd never once looked up from the ground and she'd never called down to him.

From the oak tree by the gate to the front verandah with its leafy vine and the hard green grapes that never ripened even in the hottest summer, ran a narrow pathway lined with a low box hedge. Sophie loved the smell of box leaves after rain. Even in the dry heat of December she liked to crush a few of the leaves in her hand and to sniff at the sharp pungent smell. She picked a sprig from the box hedge now and pushed it through the rope on her bundle to keep it safe for the journey.

Dad drove round from the stables. He had Daisy between the shafts of his old rattling buggy. His shirt sleeves were rolled up and his wide-brimmed hat was pushed well to the back of his head, the way he always wore it. The wrinkled skin on his neck was weathered to a dark reddish brown.

"Hop up quick, girl! I haven't got all day!"

Sophie gave her mother a hug, threw her bundle on board and climbed up after it to sit beside her father.

"Don't forget to look for letters at the gate, Tom," said Mother.

He seemed to take no notice. He clicked his tongue sharply at Daisy and shook the reins.

"Write to me, Mother! About the baby!" Sophie called back over her shoulder as the buggy lurched forward.

"Baby!" muttered her father resentfully.

Leaving a cloud of grey dust behind them, Tom Ramsdale and his daughter drove the six miles to Birregurra without speaking a word. The deeply-rutted track, often a slushy wet quagmire in winter, was now as dry as the long brown paddocks on either side. Sophie saw nothing and no one apart from a few startled magpies that flew up in front of them and a black cluster of crows cawing harshly from a gum tree. Buzzing flies hung over Daisy's back and circled the two silent figures on the buggy. Mechanically Sophie waved them away. She hardly even heard them. She felt cold and heavy inside herself in spite of the blistering heat. She hated every minute that took her further and further from home—from Mother, from the farm, from the oak tree, from Christmas, from the new baby. She hated every minute that brought her nearer to Auntie Dot and Uncle Ted with all their shadowy children and to old Grandpa Daniels down there at Stringybark Mill.

The one main street in Birregurra was almost empty. Monday wasn't a good day for shopping though the little general store stood open and waiting as usual. The women were all at home, stirring their boiling coppers or hanging out their wash. Three dairy-farmers yarned together under the shade of the Red Lion's iron verandah. One of the three looked up and raised a cheerful hand to Tom Ramsdale as he bowled past with Sophie, but Dad didn't bother to wave back. A quick curt nod of his head was his only reply. His eyes stared straight ahead. He stopped outside the railway station and waited only a bare two seconds while Sophie jumped down and pulled her bundle after her.

"Don't go near those horses, girl!" he said and without another word he clicked his tongue at Daisy again and moved away at once, turning the buggy right round in a wide dusty arc and heading straight back to the farm.

Sophie stood in the road and watched him disappear from sight. She wondered if he'd remember the letters at the farm gate a mile from the house. Slowly she crossed to Mrs Dunphy's door.

Mrs Dunphy was her mother's friend. Just about her only friend. She'd never been out to the farm. Dad had a way of making people feel they weren't welcome out there. But Mother always called in to see her once a week on shopping day, hitching up the buggy to the Dunphys' verandah post and leaving Daisy with a nose-bag full of oats to munch for half an hour or so.

Sophie knocked. The front door swung open and Mrs Dunphy's fat smiling face beamed out on Sophie.

"Mother said could you let me wait here till the train goes. I've got to go and stay with Auntie Dot down at the mill."

"Come in, love, come in! We'll have time for a nice cup of tea. So you're off to your auntie's place in the bush. That'll make a fine change for you, won't it?" And Mrs Dunphy drew Sophie into the small stuffy house that always smelled of kerosene from the lamps even when all the lamps were out. "It might be a good bit cooler down there."

"I don't want to go. I want to stay and help Mother. With the baby." Sophie's voice was thin and hard.

"I know you do, love. Your mother was telling me only last week. But she thinks it's best for you to go and I must say I agree with her, love. She's likely to have a hard time and she doesn't want you worried about it all. She's forty-two, remember."

"I know she is!" Sophie frowned as she drank her tea. "That's why I want to stay!" She wasn't at all sure why being forty-two made it harder but everyone seemed agreed that it did.

"Well, you'll just have to try and make the best of it, love. We can't always do what we want. You like your Auntie Dot, don't you?"

"She's all right. Uncle Ted's all right. But I've only met them once. And it's not home, is it?"

"Your auntie'll be glad of your help, I'm sure. How many children has she now?"

"Four."

"And your grandpa lives with them too?"

Sophie nodded.

"Well, there'll be lots for you to do, love. Your auntie must be a busy woman. Those poor devils down at the mill have a real hard life, I always reckon. I don't know how they stick it. Miles from anywhere and nothing but that wild bush all around them. Snakes and possums and kangeroos. It'd drive me mad, love, it really would. I like a nice little town. Birregurra's a good place. Always plenty going on in Birregurra."

Mrs Dunphy patted her gingham apron and smiled at Sophie.

Sophie glanced out of the window. Nothing much seemed to be going on in Birregurra as far as she could see. The street was completely empty. Even the three men outside the Red Lion had gone.

"Drink up, love, and I'll take you across to the train. It's almost time. We set our clocks here by that train to Forrest."

Mrs Dunphy took off her apron and hung it behind the kitchen door. She picked up Sophie's bundle and carried it for her. She walked briskly over to the station with Sophie beside her. The engine was hissing and steaming noisily and the two carriages behind the coal tender and the timber trucks stood quiet and empty, waiting for passengers. None came except Sophie. She climbed up reluctantly into the front carriage and the guard strolled along the platform to sell her a ticket through the open window.

"We'll soon be off, Miss," he said. "Pretty quiet today. Monday's always quiet. Looks like you're the only passenger. Hullo! Who's this?"

A plump red-faced man was pounding along the platform, a large blue carpet-bag in one hand, his black felt hat in the other. Little runnels of sweat were rolling down from his shiny bald head and into his eyes. He blinked as he ran.

"Hang on!" he panted, waving his hat up and down at the guard.

"Right you are, mate. Just in time. Hop in here. You can have this carriage all to yourself. How's that?" And the guard swung open the door of the second carriage. The red-faced man scrambled in and pulled up the carpet-bag behind him. Sophie felt relieved. She was glad he hadn't been put in with her. She'd much sooner travel alone. She waved wanly to Mrs Dunphy. The guard handed a ticket through the window to the man in the carriage next door and hurried along to his van at the end of the train. He blew loudly on his whistle and waved his flag. With a great rush of steam the train pulled slowly out of Birregurra station.

2. *Into the Forest*

The slatted wooden benches were hard and uncomfortable. Sophie sat up stiff and straight, feeling every rough jolt of the iron wheels shaking through her body. The great steam engine pounded in her ears as she watched the familiar landscape of wheat farms and dairy farms roll slowly past her. Potato paddocks, iron-roofed homesteads under the gum trees, a muddy yellow dam and a string of cattle, patches of silvery grass blowing beside the railway track — she saw it all without quite taking it in. Her thoughts were still back at home where mother would be pegging out her last line of washing in the hot dry wind.

The train stopped abruptly at Whoorel. The engine snorted and hissed. Sophie stuck her head out of the window. One solitary mail-bag flew through the air from guard's van to platform. The little station was deserted.

From the open window of the carriage next door, the other passenger's round red face craned out. And not just his face. His shoulders too and his arms. He twisted himself first one way and then the other, looking anxiously up and down the empty platform.

"Morning, Miss," said the man to Sophie with a nod.

"Good morning," said Sophie and pulled her head in again.

The train rumbled on to Dean Marsh, to Pennyroyal, to Murroon, to Barwon. Milk churns glinted in the sunlight. At every station Sophie thrust her head out through the window again. And there at every station was the round red face just a few feet away from her. There were the man's pale worried eyes searching up and down the platform. He didn't speak to her again. He hardly seemed to notice her at all. What was he looking for, she wondered? There wasn't much to see. Just one empty platform after another.

From Barwon the line turned sharply south and kept close beside the river to Gerangamete. The country was wilder here and greener. In place of the open paddocks were densely timbered hillsides and deep ferny gullies. This landscape was strange and new to Sophie. She felt more alert. She leant out of the window a little, her hair blowing back in the wind. She stared hard at the trees, straining to catch a glimpse of wallabies perhaps, or a flock of parrots, but all she could see were the thick stands of white trunks and dark trunks, rough bark and stringybark, high crowns of drooping grey-green leaves and the giant umbrellas of tree ferns by the river. She snuffed up the scent of the gum leaves and felt the cooler swish of forest air on her face. Black cinders from the engine flew into her eyes and landed in smuts on her forehead.

With a sudden lurch the train stopped at the top of the last hill before Forrest.

"Yaugher!" bellowed the guard from his van to the empty air.

The door of the next carriage swung open and the red-faced man jumped down. He dumped his blue carpet-bag on the platform.

"Thanks, mate!" he called to the guard.

The train hissed and sighed and drew away. The man clamped his felt hat onto his head and lifted the bag. Sophie looked back. The little station was not quite as empty as she'd thought. Someone was waiting there. Someone standing pressed back against the wall of the shed. Someone holding out a long hand for the blue carpet-bag. The train rounded a bend and she could see no more. The tall trees closed in again. Only a mile to go now—the last mile downhill to Forrest. Already the hop gardens were in sight on the river flat below, the green vines strung up along their wires. Sophie smoothed her tangled hair with her hands and rubbed her face on the sleeve of her dress.

Now the same questions that had been troubling her on and off all the morning pushed themselves back into her mind. Would she know Uncle Ted when she saw him? Would Auntie Dot be pleased to have her at the mill? What would the cousins be like? Would Grandpa remember her after all these years? She felt in the pocket of her dress for Mother's weekly letter to Grandpa. Whatever did her mother find to tell him every week, she wondered. Nothing ever happened at the farm.

Sophie stood up, swaying and lurching, as the train pulled into Forrest station and stopped with a final jerk. She opened the door and stepped down to the gritty platform. She held on tight to her bundle and looked quickly up and down for some sign of Uncle Ted. There was no one at all except the caretaker outside his little wooden office. Then the driver and the stoker climbed down from their engine and the guard from his van. Forrest was the end of the line. They'd have a good three hours wait till they had to swing the steam engine right round on its turntable, ready for the home run to Birregurra.

Sophie tried to look unconcerned though panic was rising inside her. She hummed a tune to herself and walked briskly along to the office door. Through the wide gaps in the paling fence she could catch her first glimpse of Forrest itself — a dusty track for the main street, a bank and a general store, a cluster of iron-roofed houses and a bullock-cart, heavily laden with timber, lumbering slowly towards the station. The sun blazed down. Sophie's mouth felt dry.

"Travelling alone, Miss?" asked the caretaker with a hint of disapproval. He was back inside his office now, pouring boiling water from the black kettle on his primus stove into a chipped enamel teapot. Sophie stood at the open doorway.

"Yes. I'm looking for my uncle. Mr Ted Blakeley."

"Ted? The blacksmith? He's just gone along to the pub, Miss. Shouldn't be long. You come in and sit here. It's cooler inside."

He pushed a pile of yellowing newspapers off a chair. Sophie sat and nervously pressed her hands together. Flies buzzed at the window.

"So you're off to the mill then, Miss?" said the caretaker, setting out a row of enamel mugs on his desk. "Been before?"

Sophie shook her head.

"But I've been up to Geelong once," she said, "to buy new shoes."

"Geelong!" grunted the caretaker in disgust. "I never could be doing with Geelong. Too big. Too noisy. The mill's a different sort of place altogether, Miss. It's a world on its own, I always say. My son's been working down there these two years. Walks right back here to Forrest every Saturday, he does, or gets a lift on top of the timber. Yes, it's a fine place all right down at that mill. Good regular money in timber, too. Them big trees'll never run out, my son reckons — not in a hundred years."

The driver and his mates came into the office for their tea. Sophie gazed around the dingy room. A faded brown map of Victorian railway lines was pinned to one wall and a calendar for 1908 on the other. A pile of dusty books of railway regulations sat on the desk. The driver lit up his pipe and the four men stood in a circle around the primus stove and drank their tea. Sophie sat alone, waiting for Uncle Ted to get back from the pub.

Mother had warned her about Uncle Ted and the pub.

"Your uncle's far too fond of the bottle," she'd said. "I don't know how Dot's put up with it all these years. Now that's a problem I've never had with your father, Sophie. Never touches a drop of the stuff. Never been inside a pub in all his life. That's something we can be thankful for. There's nothing worse in all the world than a drinking man. You'll see what I mean soon enough when you get to the mill." And Mother had shaken her head sadly.

Sophie didn't have too long to wait. She heard Uncle Ted before she saw him. His loud hearty laugh rang outside the office door and then there he was, walking in. She remembered him perfectly well the minute she saw him. His hair was red, his beard was red, his eyes were a greenish blue and his mouth was smiling. The hat on his head was a greasy black felt, the broad brim cocked up on one side. An old leather school-bag hung from his shoulder by one thin frayed strap. A billy was tied to the flap of the bag with string.

"Sophie, me darling! So here you are, all ready and waiting!" And Uncle Ted flung his great blacksmith's arms around her and squeezed her tight. He planted a wet kiss on her cheek. She could smell the beer on his breath. Something like stale stewed apples, she thought with surprise. Odd—but not unpleasant.

Uncle Ted's black-and-white sheepdog bustled in behind him and leapt all over Sophie's best dress, licking at her hands and wagging his tail excitedly. She edged back a bit towards the desk. The men around the teapot all seemed to know Uncle Ted. They shook him by the hand and clapped him on the back. They all seemed to like him too, in spite of his beery breath.

"How about a quick mug of tea, Ted," asked the caretaker, "and one for the girlie here?"

"No thanks, Fred. We've got to be on our way. We'll stop to boil up the billy a mile or so down the track. Dot's given me a stack of sandwiches here," and he tapped the bulging school-bag, "so we'll be having quite a picnic, the two of us. Come on now,

Trig," he called to the dog, "and come on Sophie, me darling, give us your bundle here." And Uncle Ted led Sophie out of the office and down the platform to the southern end where the timber tramway began.

That was the moment when Sophie first saw the horse. Her heart lurched. He stood there with his broad back to the platform's end, patiently waiting on the tram-track. His head drooped down low as if he were tired. The long heavy chains were hanging slack from the great leather collar across his shoulders. He was a big-boned draught horse, black tinged with grey, an odd splash of white down the centre of his nose and a long feathery white sock to each of his legs. His tail flicked at the flies as they settled on his rump. He tossed his head now and then to drive them away from his blinkered eyes. Sophie paused at the edge of the platform and eyed him warily. He looked docile enough but you never could be sure with horses.

"Here we are, old Clinker!" Uncle Ted called out cheerfully to the horse. "Here's poor Lily's girl come to stay at the mill!"

He leapt from the platform down to the tram-track below and tightened up the harness and the chains. Sophie hesitated for a moment and then jumped after him. Behind the big horse stood a long low truck. The bogie, Uncle Ted called it. He like the old names best. Sophie looked at it doubtfully. Clearly the bogie was built for hauling timber, not for people. There were no proper seats at all. A thick wide beam ran across each end above the axles and the wheels. Between these two beams were only the long side boards and a couple of fixed planks.

Trig sprang up on to the beam next to Clinker's black swishing tail and made himself comfortable, turning round twice before he sat. That seemed to be his usual place. Uncle Ted and Sophie perched on the back beam with her bundle and the school-bag wedged between them, their legs hanging down towards the track below. Uncle Ted released the brake and called to Clinker again. The horse lifted up his massive head and pulled forward on the chains. There were no reins to hold. Clinker knew exactly how to go, plodding slowly and steadily along his tram-track between the iron rails. Beyond the few cleared paddocks around Forrest lay the bush. Clinker plunged in, low gum leaves brushing against his coat on either side. The trees closed in around them like a long green tunnel and the township disappeared from sight behind them.

As the thick bush swallowed them up, Uncle Ted leaned back on his narrow seat, swayed from side to side and sang out happily at the top of his fine tenor voice. Sophie hung on grimly with both hands. She stared straight ahead of her at Clinker's back legs as Uncle Ted's song swirled around her.

Swing hard on your axe now boys and bring the big one down,
Strike her on her timbers boys and tip her on her crown,
Stand well clear and scuttle now — she's falling to the ground,
And the grand old queen lies dead.

Sophie gasped. The tram-rails were running right across a deep gully on a frail trestle bridge that shook and shuddered under the weight of Clinker's heavy body and the long rattling truck. She looked anxiously down into the tumbling water of the Barwon River far below as it swirled along between wet stones and dripping tree-ferns. The creaking bridge trembled but it didn't give way.

"Don't you worry now, me darling!" bellowed Uncle Ted, smiling sideways at her. "This bridge can carry huge loads of cut timber piled up high on a string of bogies. Twenty horses at a time we have going over this bridge every blessed week. So it's not going to snap under our tiny weight, is it? The old bridge sways and shakes a bit, true enough, but she's as firm as a rock, Sophie. Firm as a rock."

All the same, Sophie was glad when Clinker had reached the far side of the river and was treading on dry land once more. His big iron shoes knocked against the wooden sleepers and thudded softly on the dry earth between them. The tram-track had left the Barwon now and had turned along beside a tiny splashing creek. The dense bush opened out unexpectedly into a wide grassy clearing.

"Whoa, Clinker!" roared Uncle Ted and tugged on the bell-brake beside him. Clinker stopped. Trig jumped from his seat.

"Off you get, me darling. This is Blackberry Flat. A bit early for the blackberries but just right for boiling up our billy."

Sophie got down stiffly and looked all around her. She felt far too hot in her brown velvet dress with its long sleeves and its wide white collar. Her thick black stockings chafed her legs. Uncle Ted was unhooking the chains from Clinker's collar and leading him away from the tramway and the bogie down towards the creek. Trig was already playing happily in the water and barking at dragonflies. Clinker bent his head to drink as Uncle Ted tethered him by a long rope to a shady blue-gum.

"We'll need some shade ourselves, me darling," he said as he came back to Sophie who was still standing awkwardly beside the truck. "You just unpack these sandwiches and I'll get a good fire going."

There was a ring of blackened stones near the edge of the creek. Many another billy must have been boiled there before. Inside the ring Uncle Ted built a neat pyramid of sticks and dry leaves. He struck a yellow match against the side of his boot and set the leaves alight. Quickly he added broken twigs to keep the flame going well. He filled his black billy from the creek and planted it firmly in the middle of the fire. Sophie unwrapped the sandwiches from their pink newspaper packet.

"Do you think I could paddle in the creek, Uncle Ted?" she asked uncertainly. "I'm so hot."

"Of course you can, me darling! Off with those ridiculous stockings! I don't know what poor Lily's thinking of, sending you down to the mill with those ugly black things on your legs. Auntie Dot'll find you something cooler, I'm sure of it. None of our kids at the mill wear black stockings any more."

Sophie pulled off her shoes, peeled down her thick stockings and eased her tight garters. What a relief! In bare feet she picked her way over dry grass and sharp pebbles to the water's edge. She stepped straight in. The lively little creek surged around her white legs as her toes gripped the smooth stones. She scooped up water in her fingers to splash her face and neck. She rolled up her sleeves with wet hands and dangled both wrists in the creek. Trig danced and barked around her, splashing water all over her dress. She laughed and then stopped in surprise to hear herself laughing.

When she walked back to sit by Uncle Ted's fire, her legs dripping and gleaming, the tea was already brewed. Auntie Dot's sandwiches looked good. As she bit off her first huge satisfying

mouthful of brown bread and meat and took her first long gulp of hot tea from the enamel mug, Sophie began, for the first time that day, to feel that things might not be so bad at the mill after all.

Uncle Ted had finished his sandwiches. He stretched back on the ground for a sleep, his big brown hands limp on his chest and Trig panting quietly beside him. Sophie sat for a while looking at the lizards that scuttled over flat dry stones by the edge of the creek. Cicadas droned on all around her. Clinker moved about slowly at the end of his rope from one patch of grass to the next, chewing contentedly. Slowly Sophie's eyes began to close. She lay back against a tussock of springy pink heath. Without really meaning to, she fell asleep.

"Wake up, me darling! It's getting late! We've slept too long!" Uncle Ted's loud voice burst in on her. She sat up, startled. Already he had Clinker back between the tram-rails and harnessed to the bogie again. The fire was not only out but hissing in a pool of water. Trig was sitting up eagerly on his cross-bench. Sophie scrambled on board, shoes and stockings in her hand, and took her place next to Uncle Ted. As Clinker moved forward she pulled on her stockings and tied up her shoes. She could hardly arrive at Auntie Dot's in her bare feet. Mother would be horrified!

Though Uncle Ted was anxious to get on, it didn't seem late to Sophie. The sun was still fairly high in the sky. It might be three o'clock, perhaps, or half past. No later. They'd come a couple of miles from Forrest to Blackberry Flat. Still about four miles to go.

The air was motionless and hot as Clinker pulled his bogie further and further into the hills. He walked carefully round the sudden bends in the track. He laboured up the long gentle slopes and trotted fast down the other side with Uncle Ted's hand always ready on the brake. He crossed and re-crossed the Noonday Creek on slender swaying bridges high above the ferny gully. He rattled past a deserted sawmill, its great mound of mouldering sawdust quite overgrown with weeds.

Straight ahead along the track, Sophie caught sight of a yawning black mouth like a cave cut into the hillside. The mouth was propped open with posts and beams.

"We don't have to go in there, do we, Uncle?" she cried out

in alarm, looking around helplessly for some other way for the tram-track to go.

"Yes we do, me darling, but don't you be scared. That's a fine tunnel we've got there. She's a beauty! Bill Greenbank brought a whole tribe of miners down from Ballarat to dig it through for us. Six years ago that was. Just you wait till we get right inside, me darling. I bet you've never seen anything like it."

But inside the tunnel Sophie could hardly see a thing. It was dark and damp and cold. She could just make out the darker shape of Clinker moving on ahead of them, his chains clanking eerily. Water trickled and dripped down the slimy timbered walls on either side. The sound of Clinker's hoofs echoed all around her. Sophie shivered and gripped her bundle tighter, feeling for the little sprig of box leaves from the farm.

Now light was looming up at the end of the tunnel and soon Clinker was stepping out confidently into the hot sunshine again. Sophie blinked at its brightness. They had left the Noonday Creek behind the hill but here was the Barwon River again, narrower and faster than at Forrest, thickly overhung with bracken and ferns.

"Nearly there, me darling!" Uncle Ted stood upright on the planks and balanced precariously as the long truck clattered over yet another bridge.

The river lay on their left side now. Sophie could see a great cloud of white smoke hanging high above the trees. She could hear the heavy regular throb of a steam engine and the high-pitched whine of a saw. Clinker gave an excited whinny and quickened his pace as they burst out of the bush and into a vast ugly clearing, quite stripped of trees. Ranks of grey slab huts and houses sprawled up the bare hillside from the river, smoke belching from every iron chimney, dogs barking from every fenced back yard, white sheets flapping from every clothes line, children running and shouting along the narrow paths between the houses. Behind the grey settlement and all around it reared up the giant trunks of the big forest trees. Sophie stared.

Uncle Ted brought the bogie to a sudden halt by a landing platform. To their left, between the tramway and the river, stood a row of sheds and stables. Straight ahead was the timber mill itself, busy with moving men, noisy with screeching saws and the thudding hissing engine. Sophie looked up to the landing platform on her right. There by a high stack of sawn timber stood four red-headed children, all gazing solemnly down at her. Three of the children were girls, the eldest about her own age. The fourth was a boy. He looked very small indeed. Their eyes were a greenish blue, just like Uncle Ted's. In all her life Sophie had never seen such untidy, neglected-looking children. The girls' cotton dresses were skimpy and faded. The boy's serge trousers were torn. Their red hair flew everywhere, unbrushed and uncombed though it did look clean enough. Their feet were bare and streaked with dust. All the same, there was something very nice and comfortable about their faces, something kind and friendly. The eldest girl called down to Uncle Ted.

"You've been ages, Pa! Ma's been going real crook! We thought you'd never come."

"Ah, Queenie me darling, here we are at last! We just stopped off for a bit of a snooze at Blackberry Flat. And here's your cousin, Sophie — your poor Aunt Lily's girl from the farm. Take her along to the house now while I give Clinker a feed and a drink. He's cast a shoe a mile down the track and I'll have to make him another one before the day's over." Uncle Ted threw Sophie's bundle on to the platform and lifted her up there with both his strong hands.

Sophie looked at Queenie. She couldn't remember her at all though they must have met five years ago when Auntie Dot had brought her to the farm. She seemed to have changed. Queenie smiled at Sophie and Sophie smiled uncertainly back.

"Come on," said Queenie briskly, picking up the bundle and leading the way. Sophie caught up with her and the other three children trailed along behind.

"Is she really going crook?" asked Sophie nervously.

"Who?"

"Your mother. Because we're late."

"She *was*. But it's nothing. Her bark's worse than her bite. That's what Pa always says."

They walked between the stacks of timber and on towards the mill. The noise was deafening. Sophie clapped her hands over her ears and almost ran. The others didn't seem to notice it at all. Queenie swung up sharply to the right. There was the blacksmith's shop, a fire glowing red at the forge and two huge horses waiting outside to be shod. Sophie edged past them cautiously, keeping close to Queenie.

"We live here right next to the forge," shouted Queenie over the racket from the mill. They climbed three grey steps to a small fenced verandah. Six rabbit skins were stretched along the rail to dry. And there was Auntie Dot waiting by the door. She wasn't going crook at all. She was smiling. She looked exactly like Mother in exactly the same brown hessian apron. Even her hands seemed the same. Sophie burst into tears before she could stop herself. She flung herself into Auntie Dot's arms and buried her face in the scratchy apron.

"I didn't want to come!" she sobbed. "I didn't want to come!"

"I'm sure you didn't, dear," said Auntie Dot. "But you and Queenie'll have a wonderful summer. She's been looking forward to it so much. Now come on inside and give your face a wash. Grandpa's waiting to see you."

As Sophie came in out of the bright afternoon sun, the house seemed cool and dark. She could hardly see where she was going. Chairs and sofas reared up around her. From a far corner of the room came the old cracked voice of her Grandpa.

"Is that poor Lily's girl here at last? Come up closer, my dear, so I can get a proper look at you. My eyes aren't as good as they used to be, you know. Have you brought me my letter from Lily?"

Sophie walked carefully across the room towards Grandpa's chair. His face was old and burnt quite brown from long years in the bush. His nose was sharp and pointed and the skin was stretched tight across his cheek-bones.

"Welcome!" he croaked, holding out two shaky hands towards her. "Welcome to Stringybark Mill!"

3. *Big Horses*

It was only when Auntie Dot's family was gathered round the table for a cup of tea and a plate of hot potato scones that Sophie began to work out which cousin was which. There was no doubt about Queenie. She sat next to her father at the head of the table. Grandpa hobbled down slowly to take his place beside Auntie Dot at the foot. A big white enamel teapot, dented and chipped from years of use, stood on a cork mat by Auntie's elbow. Sophie sat at her left hand and between Sophie and Queenie was the little boy, perched up high on two fat red cushions. That must be Bertie. Queenie leant over now and then to steady his mug or to spread his potato scone with dripping and honey. Opposite Bertie were the other two girls. They looked like twins but Sophie knew that Lottie was a year older than Effie. Which one was which, she wondered, gazing from one sticky smiling face to the other.

Nothing could be more different from home than that first cup of tea around Auntie Dot's long brown table. At the farm every meal was eaten in silence apart from Mother's occasional question and Dad's abrupt answer. Sophie almost never spoke. But this table down at Stringybark Mill was alive with noise and chatter and laughter. Everyone talked at once. Sophie was stunned. She looked at them all in bewilderment. Lottie and Effie were bickering loudly but happily about who would eat the most potato scones. Uncle Ted was telling Auntie Dot at the top of his voice and right down the length of the table about a man he'd met in the pub at Forrest. Grandpa was talking up the table to Queenie, his shaky voice droning on about a trip he'd once taken to Ballarat, forty years ago or more. Queenie nodded and smiled now and then.

"Did you really, Grandpa?" she said from time to time. But most of her attention was given to Bertie who kept dribbling honey down the front of his already grubby shirt. She wiped his mouth expertly with a damp flannel and cut his potato scone into little strips so he could eat it more easily. She kept up a quiet patter of encouragement.

"That's a good boy!"
"Careful now, Bertie!"
"Down it goes!"

And then she'd look up again at Grandpa and nod.

Auntie Dot was trying to ask Sophie about her mother and the farm but with Uncle Ted's story to listen to and the tea to pour for second cups and third cups she never got very far with her questions. Sophie ate in silence, her eyes and ears trying to follow all the different conversations at once.

Suddenly a wild and terrifying sound ripped through the hot afternoon air. Everyone around the table stopped talking. Sophie froze. The sound was like the bellowing of a bull in pain. Or could it be the dreadful howling of a bunyip? The others didn't seem a bit concerned. They calmly went on eating. Sophie thought the sound would never end. On and on it boomed and roared, echoing through the bush with its terrible cry. Then, just as suddenly as it had started, it stopped. The children all began talking again.

Sophie clutched at Auntie Dot's arm. Her face was white with terror.

"Auntie! Auntie! What was it?"

Everyone laughed.

"That's just the whistle," said Auntie Dot reassuringly. "It goes off every day at half past five. The men at the mill knock off now. The day's work's over."

"But it's nothing like a whistle!" protested Sophie.

"You're right, me darling," said Uncle Ted. "It's nothing like a whistle at all. But that's what we call it all the same. It's really a fog-horn. Mr Greenbank got it from some old ship they were breaking up in Geelong. People say you can hear that blessed horn for a good twelve miles round or more. Even the sailors in the ships right out in Bass Strait reckon they can hear it when the wind's blowing off the land. Just about the whole world knows when it's knocking-off time at our mill." He was grinning with pride and tugging vigorously on his red beard.

"Is it only once a day?" asked Sophie anxiously.

"No, no!" said Grandpa, as pleased with the whistle as if he'd invented the thing himself. "*Five* times a day! There's the first blast at half past six in the mornings. That's just to test the pressure in the boiler and to tell the men to get up out of bed. Then there's the blast at half past seven. That's when work starts at the mill and the logging crews set off into the bush. The next one's at half past twelve and everyone comes home for dinner. Then half past one and the mill gets going again. And the last blast of the day goes at half past five. That's the one you heard just now. But it never goes off on a Sunday, mind, and on Saturdays the last blow is at half past twelve."

"You'll get used to it, Sophie," said Queenie. "It doesn't worry us at all."

Sophie felt sure she'd never get used to it.

"But why does it have to be so loud?" she asked.

"There's not just the men at the mill, me darling," said Uncle Ted. "There's the fallers, cutting down the big trees, miles away in the gullies, and there's the logging crews getting the logs through the bush to the tramway and back to the mill."

"And the horsemen too," put in Grandpa. "I can tell you I used to love to hear that whistle blow at the end of the day when I was out along the track there with the horses. It's a welcome sound all right."

Auntie Dot poured everyone another cup of tea.

"Queenie," she said, "you needn't go to school tomorrow. Sophie would be lonely here on her own all the morning. I've had a word with Mrs Price. You can miss the rest of this year. It's only a few more weeks anyway. When the real school opens in February, then you can start again."

"Don't you have a real school?" asked Sophie.

"We just go down to Mrs Price's house," said Queenie. "She gives us sums and spelling and reading. It's a bit of a squash with all those kids in her kitchen. But next year we're getting a real school and a real man's coming to teach us. The building's just about finished."

"Now, Queenie," said Auntie Dot, "you help Sophie unpack her things. Then you can run outside and play. We'll have a proper meal at half past six so don't go too far away."

"Wasn't that a proper meal?" asked Sophie in surprise.

"Not a meal at all, me darling," laughed Uncle Ted and the others laughed with him.

"That's just a cup of tea," explained Auntie Dot as she started carrying the sticky plates to a big tin dish on the bench by the window. She poured in hot water from a heavy black kettle heating on the fire stove and frothed it up with soap in a little wire cage on a stick. The warm soapy smell was just the same as the one that filled Mother's wash-house every Monday. Sophie felt a sharp pang of homesickness.

"Come on, Sophie," said Queenie, "I'll show you the horses."

Sophie did not move.

"Horses?" she said.

"Next door. In the blacksmith's shop. Ron's shoeing a couple of them now and Pa'll be there to do Clinker soon. Come on!"

Still Sophie did not move. She gazed down at the brown oil-cloth on the table. As she stared at the table, everyone else stared at her.

"Don't you *like* horses, Sophie?" asked Auntie Dot at last.

"Dad never lets me go near them at home. He told me to keep right away from your horses at the mill."

"Why?" asked Queenie.

"I don't know. It's just a rule. 'Don't go near the horses.' "

"Fancy a farm girl not liking horses!" said Grandpa. "Now when I was a lad in Gippsland, I could ride those horses before I could walk. I used to get up before breakfast and . . . "

"Shhhh, Grandpa," said Auntie Dot.

"Don't you ever help your father with the horses at the farm, me darling?" asked Uncle Ted.

Sophie shook her head.

"I help Mother," she said.

"In the house?" asked Auntie Dot.

"Yes—and chopping wood," she added proudly, remembering her triumph with the axe that very morning.

"Chopping wood!" exclaimed Uncle Ted. "Do you mean that poor Lily has to chop her own firewood?"

"She says it's women's work," said Sophie defensively. "She's very good at it. Every Monday morning. Dad's got the cows and the crops. He's too busy to chop wood."

There was an awkward silence around the table.

"And what horses does your father have these days?" asked

Grandpa, wanting to get away from the firewood and back to the horses.

"There's Daisy. She pulls the buggy. And Dad rides her round the fences. Then he's got a couple of big white draught horses. But he doesn't like them much. They won't do a thing he wants. Stubborn as mules, he says they are."

"And he won't let you near them?" asked Auntie Dot.

"No. I'm not allowed to go to the stables. Mother isn't either. But Dad does let her drive Daisy into town once a week. Daisy's not so bad, Dad says, but we have to watch her all the same."

"Watch her? What for?" put in Queenie.

"She might kick. Or bite. I just keep well away. Dad's always in a bad mood when he's working with the horses."

"Poor Lily," said Grandpa sadly. "She was a fine rider, too, when she was a girl. Champion of the Western District, wasn't she, Dot?"

Auntie Dot nodded.

"She never rides now," said Sophie; "I didn't know she could."

No one seemed to know what to say. The silence was uncomfortable.

Sophie wished she'd never told them about Dad and the horses.

"Do your horses kick and bite, Uncle Ted?" she asked politely when it seemed that no one else would ever speak.

"I haven't got any horses of me own, me darling. Wish I did! I'm the blacksmith. I shoe the horses. And mend the saws and chains and axes. I know every single horse on this mill as well as I know me own four kids. No, they don't kick or bite. Not if you treat them firm and gentle. That's all a good horse needs."

"If you're going to live with us through the summer, Sophie, you'll just have to get used to the horses," said Auntie Dot. "This sawmill couldn't manage without them. They're the life of the place. They haul in the logs out of the bush. And they pull the sawn timber into town. Your Uncle Ted's working with them at the forge all day long. And your Grandpa here was the head horseman till he had to stop work last year. He still goes out with them most days to give the men an extra hand. So you just can't keep away from the horses down here."

"Queenie'll show you how to handle them," said Uncle Ted.

"She's a good girl with the horses."

"I'm going to be a blacksmith," said Queenie.

"Don't be silly, dear," said Auntie Dot, smiling at her. "You're going to get married and have lots of children, like a sensible girl. Little Bertie here'll be the blacksmith, won't you, my treasure? Just like his father."

Sophie looked across at little Bertie. There was still a trickle of honey on his chin. His hair was a red glowing halo around his baby face. She couldn't quite imagine him as a blacksmith.

"You'd make a real good blacksmith, Queenie me darling," said Uncle Ted who'd noticed Queenie's disappointed face. "You've got a quiet way with the horses and you're pretty quick on the bellows too." He stood up and stretched himself. "Back to work, Dot. Back to work."

He opened the door of the house and there was Trig waiting for him on the verandah.

"Come on, Trig," he said.

"I must get that washing in," said Auntie Dot. "Lottie, you can help me. There's a good girl." She bustled off to the back yard. The girl with the most freckles on her face and hands followed her. That must be Lottie, thought Sophie.

Sophie found herself wondering if Mother had brought in her washing yet, back at the farm. The two of them always did it together on a Monday after school. They shook and pulled at the clean white sheets and folded them ready for the ironing. They piled up the shirts and the singlets in the cane basket and packed all the pegs back into the hessian bag that hung behind the wash-house door. There was something very comforting about bringing in the washing at the end of a Monday afternoon. Sophie wished she could help Auntie Dot now but Queenie was calling her to the bedroom.

The bedroom was tiny. Its space was almost filled with the two big iron beds. A row of hooks along one wall made do as a wardrobe and two orange-boxes stacked on top of each other with a gingham curtain in front served as the only chest of drawers. The two boxes seemed stuffed full of clothes already. The curtain bulged outwards.

"Where will I sleep?" asked Sophie, looking round the room.

"Lottie and Effie have the bed under the window," said Queenie. "You can sleep in this one with me."

"Is there room for both of us?" Sophie had always had a bed to herself at home. She didn't much like the idea of sharing a bed with anyone.

"Plenty of room!" laughed Queenie. "Anyway, there's nowhere else. Ma sleeps with Pa and Bertie sleeps with Grandpa. We've only got the three bedrooms. This one's the biggest by far. You can put your things in the top box. I'll shove mine along."

Queenie good-naturedly pushed her clothes to one end of the top box. Sophie untied her bundle and took out her things. She hung her two grey dresses on the hooks and put away her singlets and bloomers and thick black stockings.

"What's this?" asked Queenie, picking up the sprig of dried green leaves that had fallen to the floor.

"Just a bit from our box hedge at home," said Sophie. "I picked it this morning." She felt foolish. Queenie sniffed at the leaves.

"They smell nice," she said. "Stick them up there on the hook by the bed. I had a picture there but it fell down in a storm."

Sophie climbed on to the bed and pressed her leaves into the curved loop of the hook.

"And what's this?" Queenie was saying, holding up the white bundle of hair-rags.

"They're just for curling my hair. Mother does it every night."

Queenie's eyes opened wide in surprise and envy. She unrolled the strips of rag and looked at them one by one.

"How ever does she do it?" she asked.

"It's easy. She damps each bit of hair with a wet comb and then rolls it up tight in one of those rags. She ties a knot to stop it slipping off again. I can't do it myself, though. Do you think Auntie Dot'll do it for me?"

Queenie shook her head. "No time. She just cuts our hair off short once a month. It's no trouble. She sticks the pudding basin over our heads and cuts along the rim."

Sophie shuddered at the thought.

"And she washes our hair out in the back yard every Saturday night. With cold water too. You can hear Lottie screaming for miles around!"

Sophie pushed her bundle of rags to the very back of the orange box.

"Ma'll cut yours off short for you if you'd like," offered Queenie. "Long hair's no good in the bush."

"Maybe she'd plait it for me. That's not too much bother."

"She might," said Queenie. "We'll ask her. You'd better change out of that good dress. Put on something old. And you don't need those shoes and stockings. We just have bare feet round the mill. When we go out into the bush we have to put on our boots. Because of the snakes."

"Don't the snakes come round the mill?"

"Sometimes they do. But they're easy to see. You won't tread on one. We keep plenty of sticks ready just in case."

Sophie hadn't brought any old dresses. Mother had made her new ones and new white pinafores to keep them clean. She put on the plainest dress, unpinned the collar and rolled up the sleeves so her arms were bare like Queenie's. She took off her black shoes and stockings. The rough floor boards pricked the soles of her feet.

"Come on," said Queenie, "and we'll have a look at the horses."

Reluctantly Sophie followed her out of the house, down the verandah steps and along to the forge next door. Her bare feet dragged in the dust. Bertie was there before them, standing at the wide-open doorway and gazing into the shadowy blacksmith's shop. A dull red fire burned on the forge. A row of hammers and pliers hung from the chimney above. Someone in the shadows was hammering, metal on metal, slowly and rhythmically.

"Hullo, Ron," called Queenie from the door.

Now Sophie could see him as her eyes grew used to the dark. He was working back to back with a huge grey horse, his body pressed hard against the horse's hind leg. One hoof was gripped tight between his knees.

"G'day there, Queenie,"said Ron, looking up and speaking through a mouthful of nails.

"This is Sophie. She's my cousin from up at the farm."

"G'day there, Sophie," said Ron.

"Where's Pa?"

"He's just bringing old Clinker up from the stables."

Ron's head went down again. Sophie watched him take one

nail after another from his mouth, tap it gently into place through a hole in the bright new shoe, and then bring down the full force of his hammer to drive it firmly into the hoof. She flinched at the thought of the pain but the grey horse hardly stirred.

"Hullo there, me darlings," roared Uncle Ted's voice right behind them. Sophie jumped and turned. There he stood, wrapped in a brown leather apron, with Clinker's dark form towering up behind him. The horse looked more enormous than ever against the light. Sophie pressed herself back against the wall of the shed.

"Hold him for me, Queenie," said Uncle Ted, passing her the reins. "I'll shoe him out here. The light's better."

He strode into the shed and heaved up and down on the huge bellows till the coals glowed. He reached up for his long pliers and his short ones. He picked out four rough horse-shoe shapes from a rack on the wall and plunged them into the heart of the fire. He came outside again.

"Just hitch him to the post there, me darling," he said, and Queenie slipped the leading rein through a ring on the post and made it fast. She stroked Clinker's long black nose and the odd white splash between his eyes.

"How can she get so close?" Sophie wondered and moved still further away along the wall. Queenie left the horse and came to stand beside her.

"Right you are, old Clinker. Now let's have a look at those shoes of yours." Uncle Ted's voice was quieter now. He didn't roar. He kept on talking gently to the horse while he worked. Confidently he ran his hand down each leg in turn and lifted each hoof to tap and poke at the three old shoes.

"He needs a whole new set. They're all worn thin."

Uncle Ted pulled his small pliers from the pocket of his leather apron and tucked up the front left hoof between his knees. He set to work to prise off the old shoes and to file and rub away at the rough edges on every hoof. Softly he kept singing some bush song that Sophie couldn't quite catch.

"Don't they mind?" she asked Queenie in surprise.

"Who? Mind what?"

"The horses. Don't they mind Uncle's singing?"

Queenie laughed at the thought.

"No. They like it. He always sings when he's shoeing. He's only got three songs and we've heard them all over and over again. We're a bit tired of them but the horses don't mind. They like the old songs best."

Uncle Ted sang out louder as the shoeing got under way. Sophie watched him moving backwards and forwards between the horse and the forge. He stood at his anvil and hammered each red-hot shoe into shape with fierce blows of his hammer, sparks flying everywhere in the darkening shed. Hoof by hoof, he tapped and hammered the four shoes into place. His voice was cheerful though the song he was singing was certainly not.

Now listen me hearties and hear me sad tale,
They clapped me in prison and set me to sail
Across the wild ocean so far from me home,
To live in this land where the kangeroos roam.

The first day I got here they fixed on me chain,
And tied to a gang I worked, sunshine and rain,
We toiled up the mountains, we dug through the slime,
We hacked through great stones for the sake of one crime.

We slept on the hulk and we marched out each day,
Dry bread for our tucker, no baccy, no pay;
The troopers stood round us with whips in their hand,
And I wished that I'd never seen kangeroo land.

One day I ran off with me chain in the rear,
A'clinking and clanking so dreadful to hear,
I made for the bush and I hid there in fright
With possums and wombats all through the dark night.

And now I've been wand'ring for two years or three,
I eats fat white grubs and I drinks gum-leaf tea,
Me beard's grown so long that it scrapes on the ground,
But still I keeps moving in case I gets found.

Don't tell them you've seen me, don't split on a mate,
Just give me some tucker and show me the gate,
And if you is writing to London so fine,
Just tell dear old Polly she'll always be mine.

The mournful song came abruptly to an end. Clinker was shod. Uncle Ted straightened up slowly.

"Come here, Sophie me darling," he called.

Sophie took one step forward and stopped.

"Come on, come on!" Uncle Ted held out his large dirty hand towards her.

Slowly she moved nearer and nearer to Uncle Ted and the huge dark horse. He took her hand and placed it firmly on Clinker's neck, low down where she could easily reach. She tried to pull away but Uncle Ted held her there. With her hand in his, he stroked the warm coat. Clinker turned his head and his big wet eyes looked down at Sophie. In an instant, before she knew what was happening, Uncle Ted had lifted her bodily into the air.

"No!" she shrieked, kicking her legs wildly. "Put me down!"

Clinker snorted through his nostrils and switched his tail. His white feet shuffled.

"Easy does it, Sophie me darling. Easy does it. Keep those lolly-legs of yours still now or you'll scare the horse. Up we go!" And Uncle Ted heaved her up and astride Clinker's broad back. She sat there petrified, her hands clutching at the wiry mane.

"No! No! Please, Uncle Ted! Please take me down! I'm falling! I'm falling!"

Queenie laughed placidly and stroked Clinker's nose.

"It's all right, Sophie," she said. "You won't fall. Pa's got a good hold of you."

Ron came to the door of the blacksmith's shop to watch with Bertie.

"Just sit still, Missy," he called as Sophie squirmed about in fear. "You can't come to no harm."

Sophie sat still. She felt as if she had turned to cold stone.

"Now, me darling," said Uncle Ted, close beside her knee, "lean right down along his mane. That's it. Let your hands slip down around his neck. That's the way. He needs to get used to the feel of you. He needs to smell you. He doesn't know you yet, does he? Talk to him, me darling! Talk to him!"

Sophie's mouth was dry. She could hardly move her tongue. She couldn't think of anything to say.

"Hullo, Clinker!" she gasped out at last. Her fingers dug in tighter. She could smell the strange, strong, horsey smell of his body. She pulled herself upright again.

"That's the way, me darling. Now Queenie's coming up behind you and we'll just walk the two of you around the mill."

"No, no, Uncle Ted! Please!" She held the mane still tighter. But already Uncle Ted was swinging Queenie up onto Clinker's back. Sophie did feel a bit safer there now with Queenie's legs against her legs and Queenie's arms around her waist. But they were both so high up! The ground seemed so far away! Clinker felt as tall as a mountain.

"Don't let him move, Uncle Ted!" she cried. "Whatever you do, don't let him move!"

Clinker was moving.

"Off we go, me darlings!" Uncle Ted walked on a pace or two ahead of the horse, leading him down towards the silent mill. Clinker plodded slowly, one giant feathery hoof after the other, but to Sophie, lurching about on his back, it all seemed far too fast.

"Do stop wriggling, Sophie," said Queenie, right behind her ear. "Just grip on with your knees and keep a straight back."

"But he's not meant for riding, Queenie!" protested Sophie, her voice squeaking with terror. "He's a working horse. And he hasn't got a saddle. I'm slipping all the time!"

"Saddles!" said Queenie scornfully. "You don't need a saddle! And there's nothing wrong with having a ride on a draught horse. Men used to ride them into battle once. Didn't you even know that?"

The sun had just dipped down behind the hills and the evening sky was red. The little grey township stretching up the steep slope looked softer and less bleak. A friendly smudge of smoke hung over every iron roof. As Clinker walked patiently right around the sawmill and up and down the narrow tracks between the houses, men looked up from their gardening to wave and women called out from their front verandahs.

"Hullo, Queenie lass! Who've you got there?"

"It's Sophie," Queenie called back, "my cousin from up on the farm."

The women smiled at Sophie and inspected her with interest. Their eyes lingered on her dark cork-screw curls, tied back with the velvet ribbon, and her new grey dress that came half way down her legs. Everyone had a cheery word with Uncle Ted. A little mob of children ran along behind them with Bertie last of all.

Sophie eased herself cautiously into a new position on Clinker's back.

"Perhaps this place won't be so bad," she said to herself, "if only I can get down off this horse!"

She didn't dare to look at the ground so she looked up at the trees on the sky-line. Their great broad trunks, dark and pale, stringy and smooth, were fading bit by bit as night came on in the bush.

4. Logging

When Sophie woke up next morning she was alone in the bed and the other bed was empty. Where was Queenie? And where were Effie and Lottie? Her hair was tangled and knotted all over her head. She ran in bare feet to the kitchen. Breakfast was over. Queenie was doing the washing-up while Auntie Dot started her ironing at the kitchen table, three squat black irons heating up in turn on the fire stove.

"There you are, Sophie," said Auntie, smiling at her. "That's a good long sleep you've had. Things look better in the morning, don't they?"

"Yes," said Sophie, smiling back at her. "And I'm rather hungry. Am I too late to eat something?"

"It's never too late to eat in this house," said Auntie Dot, leaving her irons for a minute and setting out Sophie's breakfast at one end of the table. She took up a hair-brush and went to work on Sophie's hair, trying to brush out the tangles while she ate.

"I see now why your mother puts it in rags every night," said Queenie, laughing as Sophie groaned between mouthfuls.

"I think I'll plait it for you, Sophie," said Auntie Dot when the bird's nest of hair was smooth again and hanging down long and straight to well below the shoulders. "Then it'll be out of your way in the daytime and it won't get all in a mess at night."

Sophie felt odd with two tight plaits pulling on her head in place of the usual loose curls.

"We'll need our boots on today," said Queenie, excited at the prospect of this unexpected holiday stretching for weeks ahead of her. "Grandpa's going to take us out into the bush to watch the logging."

"Grandpa? Isn't he far too old to go out into the bush? He'd never walk far with that stick of his."

"You just wait and see," said Auntie Dot, thumping down her heavy iron on a folded sheet. "He likes to look the poor old invalid here in the house but once he's out along that track he's as spry as a man half his age. You go and get washed and dressed now.

You can have a dish of warm water outside the back door. Grandpa will be ready for you in half an hour or so."

As soon as she was dressed, Sophie stood with Queenie on the little verandah to wait for Grandpa. The dried rabbit-skins were piled in one corner and two sleek ferrets scuttled about in a metal cage. Sophie moved a bit further away from them though she knew they couldn't get out. The morning air was fresh. The pleasant smell of new-baked bread wafted up from the bake-house below. The saws at the mill screamed and whined and the steam engine that drove them hissed and pounded.

"Did that whistle blow this morning?" asked Sophie, suddenly remembering her terror of the night before.

"Yes. Twice. Didn't it wake you?"

"I didn't hear a thing."

"That's good," laughed Queenie. "I knew it wouldn't scare you for long. Everyone gets used to it."

Sophie's eyes ran over the untidy rows of huts and houses and up to the great ring of giant trees that circled them round. What kinds of trees were they, she wondered. Gums, most of them, of course, but what sort of gums? How would she ever learn their names? Down by the mill, a team of six horses was just setting out for Forrest with a load of sawn timber stacked on the long trucks behind them. The horses plodded, nose to tail between the tram rails, each one linked to the next by swaying jingling chains. The team and the bogies disappeared into the bush, making for the tunnel half a mile away. A sudden muffled shout went up from the three men perched on top of the load. Were they just greeting someone along the track or were they warning someone to get out of their way?

A few minutes later two figures emerged from the bush, stepping wearily from one thick wooden sleeper on the tram-track to the next. They paused as they reached the clearing and gazed around the township with a bewildered air. The man in front was tall and lumbering with broad solid shoulders and long gangling arms. Big as he was, the clothes he wore seemed far too large for him and far too hot for a day like this. His black coat hung around him in loose baggy folds. His trouser cuffs trailed in the dust. He pulled the coat off, flung it over one arm and stood in his shirt sleeves. His hair was dark and well-sleeked down with oil. His beard was long and scraggy. The second man stood a pace or two behind him. He was short and plump with a round red face and a balding head. He was fanning himself weakly with a black felt hat. At his feet lay a blue carpet-bag. Bulging.

"Look!" exclaimed Sophie, pointing down at the men.

"What is it?"

"That man with the bag. I saw him yesterday. On the train. He got off at Yaugher. Who is he, Queenie? And who's that other one? He looks like a scarecrow with those floppy clothes on!"

"Never seen them before. But I know who they are all right. Just a couple of hawkers. We get a lot of them down here. Every couple of weeks or so one of them turns up. They always have a bag like that—or a flat one that opens out. Ma'll be pleased to see them."

"What's in the bag?"

"The things they're selling. Don't you get hawkers up at the farm?"

Sophie shook her head.

"We've got a notice on the gate that says 'No Hawkers'. I'm not too sure what they are."

"They just tramp along the country roads from town to town. And then they go round from house to house. They stand at the front door and open up their bags. Then you choose what you want to buy. I love looking in to see what they've got."

"What do they sell?"

"Just about everything! Bootlaces and buttons and pegs and needles. Black stuff to clean the stove with. Shoe polish and hair-brushes and ribbons. Cough mixture. Ointment for the horses. Saucepans, sometimes, and pieces of new cloth. Ma always buys something. She even bought a book once."

"A book!"

"It's still round the house somewhere. *Jessica's First Prayer* it was called. She bought it for Pa but he didn't take to it. I don't think these two men have got books. The bag's not big enough."

The hawkers were clearly strangers in the place. They didn't seem to know where to begin. Sophie and Queenie could see them arguing about it, pointing first up the hillside to the houses and then along the river to the mill. They sat on a log and the big man pulled a sheet of paper from his pocket. They bent their heads down over the paper and then, once more, began to gaze this way and that around the settlement.

With a sudden decision, the two men leapt to their feet, clamped their hats on to their heads and started walking again. They came straight along the tram-track to the mill and up the slope to the blacksmith's shop.

"They're coming here!" said Sophie.

"That's funny. They usually start on the other side. We're at the end of the round. There's something very strange about those two hawkers!"

"Perhaps they want to see Uncle Ted."

"No, no. Not Pa. He never sees them. It's only the women that buy things."

"Here they are, anyway." Sophie felt oddly alarmed.

"Good morning, Miss," the big man called up to Queenie, lifting his hat an inch or two and pushing it down again on the back of his head. The red-faced man stared hard at Sophie. She knew he was trying to remember where he'd seen her before. He had half a smile on his face and half a frown.

"I'll just get Ma," offered Queenie.

"No, no. Don't trouble your mother, Miss. You can help us, I'm sure. We're looking for a Mr . . . Mr . . . He fished in his pocket for the piece of paper again. "A Mr . . . yes, here we are, Greenbank. Do you know where he lives, Miss? These mill houses all look the same to me."

"Mr Greenbank? He's the boss! *He* won't be buying anything. Why don't you just start anywhere?"

"It's Mr Greenbank we want to see, Miss. He's expecting us, see."

He waved the paper at Queenie.

"You won't find him up in his house," she said. "He'll be down at the mill. He's always the first on the job every morning. But you'll have to shout to make yourself heard in there. The saws make such a racket. Just ask any of the men. They'll show you which one he is." She pointed down to the shuddering sawmill. White smoke was billowing from its chimney and white steam oozing through the cracks in the roof.

"Come on there, Drake!" said the big man sharply. "No dawdling and gawping! Pick up that bag!" And with another brief lift of his hat to Queenie, he turned and strode off down towards the mill. The red-faced man had been wiping his sweating forehead with a dirty handkerchief. Now he snatched up the bag and hurried down the hill.

"Wait on, Mr Hooker!" he called out. "I can't keep up with you. Me legs are wore off! You never said it was so far!"

The two men turned by the log-landing and disappeared into the mill. Five minutes passed. The whine of the saws and the beat of the engine never paused for a second. Then the two men came out again with a third man walking between them.

"That's the boss," said Queenie. "Mr Greenbank. Grandpa calls him Bill but no one else does. He's a good boss. Owns this whole mill."

Mr Hooker held the blue bag now. Drake was nearly running as he tried to match his short steps to the boss's long ones.

"Where are they going?" asked Sophie.

"Up to the Greenbanks' house, I suppose." Queenie frowned as she watched them making their way between the fences and up to the boss's grey house at the top of the township. His house was much the same as all the others. "I wonder what they're selling?"

"Perhaps they're just old friends. Dropped in to see him."

"No, Sophie. They can't be his friends. They couldn't even remember his name. They had it on that bit of paper."

The three men climbed the steps to Mr Greenbank's verandah and pushed open the front door.

"I don't think I like those hawkers!" said Queenie, still puzzled and frowning. "They're up to no good!"

"Queenie! Sophie! I'm ready for the bush! Off we go!" and Grandpa stepped out just behind the two cousins in his moleskin trousers, his red shirt, his wide-brimmed hat and black boots so solid that Sophie wondered how he could lift his feet off the ground. She could hardly recognize him as the frail old man of last night. His stick tapped firmly on the verandah floor as they set off.

Uncle Ted was working away on a broken saw in the blacksmith's shop. Trig sat beside him, watching every move. Grandpa led the girls down behind the mill, around the enormous yellow sawdust heap and on to the tramway running east along the river.

Sophie trod carefully on each of the flat sleepers in turn but Queenie danced along the rails, balancing first on one side and then on the other, chattering as she ran. The dark feathery green leaves of the wattle trees and the paler branches of the blue-gum saplings crowded up close to the track and brushed against Grandpa's hat as he stooped beneath them. A few yards away on their left the river sang and swirled under wet tree-ferns and clumps of trailing maiden-hair. As they drew further and further away from the deafening pulse of the mill, the bubbling river seemed louder. For the first time Sophie began to hear the birds clearly. They were all around her in the shaking leaves—whistling, calling, fluttering, squawking. The trees flashed with the colours of their wings—red and green, blue and yellow, white and black. Grandpa made Queenie stop her talking and leaping. He knew the names of all the birds. There were blue wrens, honeyeaters, silver-eyes, willie-wagtails and, brightest of all, the crimson rosellas, the lorikeets and the gang-gang cockatoos. Sophie looked around her in amazement. She had never seen so many birds or heard such sounds. They seemed oddly tame and went on with their noisy foraging and feeding as if no one were there to watch them.

Sophie paused to pick a sprig of pink heath bells and a purple chocolate flower with its strange vanilla scent. Queenie pulled at a red and yellow strand of "eggs and bacon" to trail in her hair.

"Come on, girls, come on," said Grandpa. "Leave those flowers for the way back. I want to get to the logging."

He pressed ahead along the tram-track, his stick swinging rhythmically, his legs moving so fast that Sophie found it hard to keep up with him. Auntie Dot was right. He wasn't a dying old man after all.

The track climbed away from the river and ran along a ridge. They came to a high trestle bridge that spanned the gully. Sophie walked more slowly here. She thought for a minute that she could feel the bridge moving beneath her but it stood on its great tree-trunk pillars as firm as a rock. Queenie skipped to the side and peered down into the swirling water far below and the mass of dripping tree-ferns. Sophie kept well to the middle of the tram-track, hardly even daring to turn her head to look along the deep gully to left or to right. After the bridge came a tunnel, its walls damp and streaming with water like the one she'd been through yesterday but shorter, broader and not so dark. Then another bridge. Grandpa turned away from the main tramway to follow a branch line up a little creek that flowed into the river from their right.

The bush was even denser here. Sophie gasped as two big kangeroos bounded suddenly across the track ahead of them. They looked quite as startled as she was.

"This is Coldwater Creek," said Queenie. "We often see kangeroos up this way. I've seen koalas too. They don't like to come too close to the mill. It's too noisy."

"We'll hear the logging crew at work in a minute," said Grandpa. "They can't be far off now."

Sophie wasn't quite sure what kind of sound she should be listening for but when she heard it she recognized it at once. The sharp echoing thud of an axe. As they moved further up the creek she could hear the rasp of saw blades and the shouting of the horseman to his team.

"Whoa there, Sandy! Come on now, Bella! Heave away, Clinker! Up we come! Up we come!"

"Nearly there, Sophie," said Grandpa. "That's Ray Sanders you can hear bellowing away at the horses. He bellows a bit too much for my liking but he's good with the horses all the same. I taught him all he knows. Ten years he worked under me here and I made a fine horseman of him, though I say it myself. But he still bellows a bit too loud. Those horses can hear all right without a lot of bellowing."

At a wide bend in Coldwater Creek, the tramway left the mushy bottom of the gully and climbed higher along the steep side of the hill. Down below by the water's edge amongst the tree ferns, one team of horses was pulling on a log so huge that Sophie could hardly believe it had ever stood upright on the earth. The six heavy horses were linked to each other with long chains that were strained to full stretch now as Ray urged the team forward along the gully floor and up the slope.

"Where are they dragging it to?" asked Sophie.

Queenie knew all about it.

"They're bringing it up to that landing platform by the tram-track. We'll get a good view from here."

The great log swung from side to side behind the horses, gouging out a wide passage as it was dragged through the mossy earth, flattening ferns and tiny saplings in its path.

"G'day there, Harry!" the horseman called up to Grandpa with a wave of his whip. "You've come at just the right time. I could do with a hand down here."

Grandpa passed his walking-stick to Queenie. He seemed to walk quite as well without it as he hurried down to the horses. He took hold of Sandy's bridle in front and urged him fowards while Ray went to the back of the team and shouted from there. The log inched its way along the gully and up to the landing platform. The six horses were snorting and breathing heavily, their nostrils open wide, their flanks running with sweat. Mud covered the thick feather of hair that hung from their fetlocks. Sophie edged further away as the horses came closer.

At the landing platform the men unchained the log and managed to manoeuvre it gradually into position. They fixed stout ropes to a couple of tree stumps on the far side of the tram-track, passed them over the rails and under the log, and then back over the platform and the timber truck to the horses. With skids cut from saplings to form a ramp tucked under the log and up to the platform, everything was ready at last for the big pull.

Ray gave the word. The men from the logging crew shouted and swore. The horses heaved and strained. Inch by inch the log crept up the skids to the platform. Inch by inch it rolled across the platform to the truck. With a sudden rush the men just stopped it in time from rolling off the truck on the other side. Grandpa gave a shout of triumph as the massive log was roped and chained into place for the ride back to the mill.

"Good work, Ray!" he called to the horseman. "That's a great team you've got there. I can remember the days when we used to use bullocks for that job. Stupid lumbering beasts they were too. Give me horses any day. Horses can think!"

Sophic had bccn watching from well back against the trunk of a tall brown stringybark. The bark itself, like rough coir matting wrapped around the tree, was splitting off in long stringy hanks that rubbed against Sophie's bare arms. She felt scared by the noise of bellowing men and labouring horses but Queenie was quite untroubled by it all. They both heard words flying through the air that Sophie had never heard before. Something told her that they weren't the sort of words to try out in Auntie Dot's kitchen or in Mother's either, for that matter.

Everything was quieter now. The men from the logging crew flopped back on the bracken for a rest and a smoke while Grandpa and Ray harnessed up the string of horses to the truck, one behind the other along the tramway. Grandpa moved down the row from one horse to the next, speaking quietly to each in turn.

"Well done, Sandy!" he said, stroking the long brown nose of the leading horse. "Good girl, Bella! That's the way, Diamond! You're a beauty, Flick, a real beauty! Good lad, Silver! And here's my dear old Clinker! Well done, Clinker!"

Sophie watched as Grandpa stretched right up, pulled Clinker's head down towards him and whispered into one black pricked ear. Clinker whinnied happily and tossed his mane from side to side. His big brown eyes, shaded by the blinkers, turned towards Sophie where she stood pressed against her tree.

"He remembers you, Sophie!" cried Grandpa. "He remembers you! Come over here now and talk to him."

Reluctantly Sophie walked towards the horse. Grandpa took her hand and lifted it up in his to stroke Clinker's dark warm coat, still damp with sweat. Clinker looked down at her and nuzzled into her shoulder. Her feet wanted to spring back in alarm but Grandpa held her firm.

"Talk to him, girl," he said.

"Good morning, Clinker," said Sophie, her voice squeaking oddly.

"That's the way," said Grandpa. "Clinker knows you now. He remembers your voice from yesterday. There's nothing to be scared of now, is there?"

Sophie glanced down at Clinker's four enormous hoofs, planted firmly on the ground. She wasn't so sure.

Ray Sanders had climbed up to the very top of the log with two of the men beside him. They sat there with their feet dangling. Ray released the brake and shouted to the horses.

"Gee up there! Off we go!"

The six horses bent their shoulders and strained forwards on the load. Slowly the bogie began to roll. The horses quickened their pace a little. They knew they were making for home, back along the tramway to Stringybark Mill.

"Can we watch the fallers now, Grandpa?" asked Queenie. Two men from the logging crew were up on their feet again and working their way down towards the creek. They had their next tree picked out already — a huge giant with solid buttresses round its base and stretching up and up into the hot blue sky.

"Right you are, girl. I'd like Sophie to see a good fall. Come on. We'll follow them down. That's a fine mountain ash they've got there."

Sophie sat with Grandpa and Queenie on a mossy rock by the water's edge. A tree-fern drooped over their heads and kept off the sun. The two fallers were walking round the mountain ash, sizing her up and discussing which way they wanted her to fall. Sophie's eyes moved anxiously from the tree's vast base, up the trunk to the distant crown of grey-green leaves.

"How can they be sure which way it will fall, Grandpa?" she asked.

"It all depends on where they make their first cut. That's the side where she'll come down. They find somewhere with a bit of space for the fall. You just look now, Sophie. That butt's far too big for the saw. They'll have to go up the trunk a bit before they start. Watch!"

Sophie watched. The two men were cutting small footsteps up the side of the tree and knocking in pegs made from saplings. They climbed the footholds, pulling out one peg at a time behind them and driving it into the trunk higher up. A good seven feet above the ground they laid a plank across two level pegs to make a platform.

"They'll work from there to start with," said Grandpa. "Ernie's left-handed and Steve's right-handed. That way they can work better as a pair. They'll chop the scarf out first. There they go!"

"Whale away!" shouted Steve, lifting his axe high above his shoulder with both hands and bringing it down against the tree with a sharp resounding whack. The axe bit into the wood and the white chips flew. As Steve's axe swung up again, Ernie's axe flashed down from above and cut into the tree at exactly the same place. The two men worked together in a steady rhythm, their axes rising and falling in turn as they cut into the tree. The wide deep gash of the scarf reached almost to the centre of the tree. Sophie could clearly see the rings in the wood from where she was sitting—year after year of its growth.

"Now they strip the bark," said Queenie.

The men began to cut and pull off the layer of bark, leaving a clean white band on the trunk of the tree. They made new footholds and moved their platform right round to the other side, stripping the bark as they went. Directly opposite the scarf, Steve's axe made a new straight cut to take the blade of the saw. The men put down their axes and took up the long cross-cut saw. They fitted it carefully into the slit.

"Whale away!" shouted Steve again and he pushed forward on the saw.

Ernie pulled back hard at his end and the saw's teeth began to eat into the timber. Steve leaned backward and Ernie lunged forward. Their rhythm got under way again. Now Sophie could hear the singing rasp of the saw as the two men almost danced on their platform, swaying backwards and forwards up there against the broad trunk.

The saw worked its way into the heart of the tree and came nearer and nearer to the scarf on the other side. The men paused now and then to drive wedges into the cut to lift the weight of the trunk off their saw and to tilt it slightly so they could steer its fall. Only one narrow inch was left now between the saw blade and the scarf. The men moved more slowly. Sophie held her breath. The saw broke through.

For a long long second nothing happened at all. The tree still stood upright, balanced precariously on its butt. Then slowly, with a loud crack, the great tree began to fall.

"Timber!" shouted Steve triumphantly and leapt from the platform right down to the ground below. Ernie shouted and jumped at the same instant. Sophie heard another of those words she'd never heard before. Queenie laughed.

"There she goes!" cried Grandpa, hopping up in excitement to watch the fall. Sophie stood beside him and grabbed onto his arm.

Boughs snapped and leaves swished and tore as the mighty giant toppled to the earth. Sophie watched in amazement. It all seemed to her like something in a dream. She couldn't quite believe her eyes. Her ears were full of the fearful noise. Now the men ran to the tree where it lay stretched out along the ground and began to clamber all over it with their axes in their hands.

"That's a fine fall!" said Grandpa in admiration. "And no sailors either!"

Sophie looked around her in bewilderment.

"Sailors?" she said.

Queenie laughed again.

"That's just what they call the branches that get all tangled up in other trees on the way down," she said.

"Dangerous things, sailors," said Grandpa. "These blokes know what they're doing."

Sophie sighed.

"I wish they didn't have to cut down such a lovely tree," she said.

"Business is business, Sophie," said Grandpa. "We've all got to make our living. The mines up in Ballarat need our timber for their props and their poppet legs. The fencers need these trees and the bridge-builders need them too. We can't cut them down fast enough. Everyone's crying out for more timber. But you don't need to worry, Sophie. Just look at all those trees. Thousands and thousands of them. Messmate and manna gums. Mountain ash and blackwood. We can take all we want and there'll still be thousands more."

Sophie wasn't convinced. She could only look sadly at the magnificent tree lying dead on the ground, the two fallers climbing along its length, hacking off enormous boughs and branches till the trunk was stripped and bare.

"Well," said Grandpa. "That's that. We'd better be making tracks. Come on!"

Sophie and Queenie climbed the steep slope, one on each side of him, till they reached the tramway again.

"Hullo!" Grandpa's voice had suddenly changed. He was talking to himself. "That's funny!"

"What's funny?" asked Queenie. She and Sophie looked where Grandpa was looking — straight down the tramline.

"There's the boss," said Grandpa, "and a couple of new blokes with him too. I wonder what they want. I just hope they're not looking for work, that's all. We've got no jobs to spare at Stringybark Mill!"

Grandpa looked quite fierce as Mr Greenbank and the two strangers came nearer.

"They're not looking for work, Grandpa," said Queenie, laughing up at his cross face. "They're just a couple of hawkers. We saw them turn up at the mill this morning. They were looking for Mr Greenbank but I told them he'd never buy anything."

"They don't look like hawkers to me!" muttered Grandpa.

"G'day there, Harry!" called Mr Greenbank cheerfully. His big white collie dog was bounding along in front of him. Mr Greenbank came up to Grandpa and shook him by the hand. The two new men hung back a bit. Mr Greenbank smiled down at Sophie.

"So you've got another little grand-daughter with you today, Harry. The wife told me she'd come."

"That's right, Bill," said Grandpa, looking less suspicious now. "This is my dear Lily's girl from up at the farm. She's come to stay with us right over Christmas. Sophie, this is our boss, Mr Greenbank."

Sophie held out her hand, not quite sure if it was the right thing to do. Mr Greenbank grasped it firmly. She looked up at him.

Mr Greenbank seemed much older than Uncle Ted but not nearly as old as Grandpa. He was a tall thin man with a lined brown face. His bushy black beard was sprinkled with silvery hairs. He was dressed like most of the other men who worked at the mill in a blue shirt and black serge trousers with a buttoned waistcoat over the shirt. But he had something that none of the other men had — a thick gold watch chain draped across his narrow chest. The watch itself lay buried deep in the waistcoat pocket and made an odd round bulge in the cloth. Mr Greenbank was still smiling at her, wrinkling up his eyes.

"Pleased to meet you, Sophie. You must come up to the house and say hullo to the wife. She likes to know all the kids around the mill, doesn't she, Harry?"

Grandpa nodded.

"Mrs Greenbank's a real good friend to all the kids," he said. "No favourites. Treats them all the same. That's what I like."

Now Grandpa let his eyes wander past Mr Greenbank to the two strangers.

"You've got company today, Bill," he said. He lowered his voice. "Not looking for work, I hope."

Mr Greenbank laughed.

"No, no, Harry. Nothing like that at all. But you must meet them." He turned and beckoned the strangers forward.

"This is Jack Hooker from up Wangaratta way. Knows a lot about horses. And here's his mate, Norm Drake." Now Mr Greenbank leant one thin hand on Grandpa's shoulder. "And this," he went on, "is Harry Daniels. Used to be our head horseman. Backbone of the mill. Still lends a hand with the horses, don't you, Harry? And these two girlies here are his grand-daughters. Not sisters, mind. Cousins. Queenie and Sophie."

Mr Hooker shook hands with Grandpa.

"Pleased to meet yer," he said. "Used to be a horseman meself, once upon a time. We seen these two kids up on yer verandah. Hullo there!" And he nodded to the girls.

Norm Drake jerked his head briefly but did not speak. He was out of breath from the walk and his round red face was streaming with sweat. He stared at Sophie, still puzzled.

"Warming up," said Grandpa as Norm Drake dragged his shirt sleeve across his forehead. "Just looking round, Mr Hooker, is that it?"

Before Jack Hooker could answer, Mr Greenbank spoke up for him.

"That's it, Harry. Just looking round. Wanted to see our big horses at work so I brought him and his mate out along the tram-track. We passed Sandy and a few of the others back there near the mill. Good big log in tow too. But that one by the creek looks even bigger. What a beauty!"

Mr Greenbank strode down to the newly-fallen tree and inspected it with approval.

"Nice job, boys," he said to the fallers who were stacking the lopped branches. "A good clean cut."

He lifted his head and looked up carefully into the tall trees all around.

"And no sailors either," he added with a happy grin.

Jack Hooker and Norm Drake didn't seem much interested in the huge log lying stretched out on the ground. Sophie thought they didn't even seem impatient for the horses to get back from the mill. They were looking intently at the tram-track, pacing out the width of the sleepers, tapping at the rails with a hammer, peering right under the wheels of the long empty bogie that stood there waiting for the next load.

"Good solid track yer've got here, Mr Greenbank," said Jack Hooker.

"We can wander up the main line now and take a look at the steam winch if you like," offered the boss. "There's another team of horses working up there too."

"No, no! We've seen enough, haven't we, Mr Hooker?" said Norm Drake quickly. He looked as if he was anxious not to do too much more walking in the heat.

"Yep. Must be getting back, Mr Greenbank. Taken up enough of yer time." He dropped his voice a little but Sophie could still hear him perfectly clearly. "There'll be no problems, Mr Greenbank. No problems at all. She'll be right!" And Mr Hooker rubbed his hands together. He looked almost excited.

The boss set off back along the track with Jack Hooker loping along beside him and Norm Drake half running to keep up. Grandpa gazed after them, a small frown between his eyes. He didn't speak.

"*Why* are they just looking round?" asked Queenie.

"I wish I knew," said Grandpa, scratching his white head. "They're up to no good, those two chaps. But I can't fathom it out at all."

5. *The Search*

"Bertie! Bertie!"

Auntie Dot's voice was sharp and anxious. She called again and again from the front verandah, leaning over the rail and waving a white tea-towel up and down.

"Queenie! Sophie! Where's Bertie?"

Queenie saw her at once and came running up the hill with Sophie just behind her. It was the morning after their walk along the tram-track to watch the big tree fall. They'd been sliding down the yellow heap of sawdust behind the mill. Auntie Dot's voice was completely drowned by the pounding of the steam engine that drove the saw and the whine of the saw-blades. But the waving tea-towel was a family signal that Queenie knew well.

"Something's wrong, Sophie! Come on! Ma needs us!" she'd shouted. Quickly she'd brushed the powdery sawdust from her dress and started running.

"What is it, Ma?" she called, bounding up the steps.

"It's Bertie! He's gone! He was playing with his little train out the back and now he's gone! I've been calling and calling."

Bertie's wooden engine lay on its side in the dust outside the back door. Uncle Ted had made it for him out of a nice piece of blackwood. It had a fat chimney and a round boiler but no wheels.

"I'll get Pa," offered Queenie.

"No, no. Not yet. We've got to search the settlement ourselves first. Bertie's probably just wandered off into someone else's back yard. He'd never hear me over the noise of the mill."

"Where will we look?" asked Sophie.

"I'll take Lottie and Effie with me," said Auntie Dot, untying her apron and smoothing her hair. "We'll go from house to house and ask. I want you two to look in the forge and the shops. Go right into the mill, too, and don't forget the stables and the billiard shed. I've caught him in there more than once. You'd better be back here in ten minutes. If we haven't found him by then, we'll have to call in the men."

Queenie took Sophie's hand and ran with her into the forge

beside the house. Uncle Ted and Ron were making sparks fly in the gloom as their hammers fell, one after the other, on a red-hot scythe on the anvil. The two men didn't even look up to see Queenie scanning all the dark corners and darting out again.

"He's not there," she said and ran full tilt down to the bake-house with Sophie beside her.

"Have you seen Bertie?" Queenie asked, peering in at the open door. Mrs Schwartz smiled at her from behind the rows of long brown loaves.

"No, dear. He hasn't been here. Try next door," she said.

Sophie wanted to linger in the bake-house but Queenie pulled her on.

"We've lost Bertie," she said to the butcher in the shop next door. "Have you seen him anywhere?"

The butcher flapped at the flies that buzzed around his meat and shook his head.

Two or three women were waiting their turn in the general store beside the butcher's shop when Queenie and Sophie burst in.

"Have you seen Bertie? He's wandered off," said Queenie.

No one had seen him.

Sophie ran her eyes carefully along the shelves of interesting canisters and jars behind the counter.

"He won't be there!" laughed Queenie. "Come on. We'll try the mill."

With their hands clamped over their ears to shut out the thudding and screeching noise of the mill, they walked boldly inside. Mr Greenbank himself was working on the big saw. He waved cheerfully to the girls.

"Have you seen Bertie?" bellowed Queenie right into his face.

"No!" he bellowed back. "Have a look round! But keep well away from this saw!"

Sophie followed Queenie timidly as she poked in behind the stacks of sawn planks and the piles of heavy logs. Not a sign of Bertie. Queenie jerked her head towards the door and Sophie scuttled out after her, thankful to escape from the din.

"Now the stables," said Queenie, dashing on ahead.

The stables stood empty at this time of the day, their wide doors flung open to let the fresh air into the twenty stalls. Sophie didn't mind walking in there now that all the horses were out in the bush. She liked the smell of hay and the shadowy coolness away from the hot sunlight. Des, the stable-boy, had already swept the floor clear and was filling up the drinking troughs with water from the river, bucketful by bucketful. He looked up at Queenie and Sophie and grinned.

"We've lost Bertie," said Queenie. "Has he been down here with you?"

Des's grin faded. He looked worried.

"No. Been here all morning. Haven't seen him at all. What about the river?"

"What about it?" Queenie's voice was fainter as an awful thought struck her.

"He could've fallen in. There's some deep pools."

Sophie gasped.

"We'd better go and look," she said.

"I'll do it," offered Des, pulling off his boots and making for the water. "I'll work downstream first. You'd better tell your Pa."

Queenie nodded.

"We've just got to look in the billiard shed first. Then we'll tell Pa. Thanks, Des."

Des stepped right into the water and began to wade downstream, balancing sometimes on the flat wet stones and sometimes standing on the gravelly bottom.

"Bertie! Bertie! Coo-ee!" he called, bending down to look right under the tree-ferns that trailed their leaves in the water.

From the outside, the billiard shed looked much the same as all the other buildings in the settlement — rough splintery palings for walls, an iron roof painted red, small windows on every side, a round tank at the back and a verandah across the front. But where all the houses faced downhill to the river, only the billiard shed and the stables faced up the hill.

Hesitantly Sophie followed Queenie through the door. There was no one inside. A funny smell of stale tobacco hung in the air and clung to the gingham curtains. The dirt floor was packed hard. In the centre of the room stood a long table covered with green baize. A box of balls and a few smooth tapered sticks lay underneath. A row of upright chairs was ranged along each side wall and at the far end was a counter covered with brown oil-cloth.

Sophie was puzzled. Her eyes wandered from the green table to the mysterious sticks and back again.

"What's it all for?" she asked.

"It's a game. Billiards. The men all come in here every night and play it with these sticks and balls. They have a bit of a sing-song too. Pa's really good at that. Sometimes they sit round a camp-fire by the edge of the river. We can hear them talking and singing right up at our house. Pa says they go on till three in the morning."

"Mr Greenbank should stop it," said Sophie, shocked at the very thought of such late hours. "It's his mill."

Queenie laughed.

"He's generally there himself. He likes a good sing-song and a yarn with the men. The noise never keeps me awake but Ma gets a bit cross."

"Can't she come down too with Uncle Ted? To play this game and sing the songs?"

Now Queenie looked shocked.

"No, no. That sort of thing's just for the men. Everyone knows that. The women never come in here. Except at Christmas."

"What happens then?"

"You'll see. It's something good."

Suddenly Sophie heard Des's distant voice calling for Bertie.

"Hurry up, Queenie!" she said. "We've wasted too much time in here."

Auntie Dot was back at the house just before them. Her face was pale now.

"He's gone!" she said. "He's really gone this time. I've been into every blessed house at this mill."

"Des is searching the river," said Queenie.

Auntie Dot shuddered.

"We'll have to get in the men," she said and hurried off to the forge.

"Bertie's lost, Ted!" she called. "We've searched the whole place. He's gone!"

The hammers were still.

Queenie and Sophie ran in after her.

"And Des said to tell you he's working downstream. There's some deep pools," said Queenie.

"The river!" exclaimed Uncle Ted. "I'll get Mr Greenbank to blow the whistle. We'll need all the men back from the logging. Make some tea, Dot. It could be a long search. Come on there, Ron."

The two men rushed to the mill. Within seconds the saw had stopped. The terrible whistle screeched out its wild signal of distress. Three short blasts, three long, three short. Mr Greenbank led all his men out of the mill and began sending them off into the bush, fanning out from the settlement. Ron took the tram-track towards the long tunnel and Forrest. Uncle Ted went the other way to Coldwater Creek to meet the logging crew and bring them into the search. Mr Greenbank himself stayed near the mill, waiting for news.

Auntie Dot had her apron on again. Sophie and Queenie helped her to put all the black kettles on the stove, ready for making tea.

"Can't we go and look for Bertie too?" begged Sophie. She felt restless, cooped up in the hot kitchen when all the men were combing the bush. Even the older boys from Mrs Price's school had joined in now.

"You'd only get lost yourself, Sophie," said Auntie Dot. "That'd make more trouble for everyone."

"No, I wouldn't!" Sophie was indignant.

"I wouldn't either!" said Queenie stoutly. "Pa's shown me how to look after myself in the bush. I know what to do."

Auntie Dot was too worried and wearied to argue with them.

"All right," she said. "But put your boots on first. There could be snakes about. And stick to the track or the river. Don't just wander off into the trees."

Sophie and Queenie didn't wait for Auntie Dot to change her mind. As soon as their stockings and boots were on, they dashed out of the house. At the foot of the steps they stopped and looked around them.

"Which way will we go?" asked Queenie, suddenly unsure of herself.

"Which way do you think Bertie's gone? Where does he like to go?"

"He'd probably follow Grandpa down the tram-track to find the horses. He loves the horses. But Pa's gone that way already."

"Let's go after Uncle Ted, then. He's walking fast to reach the men. We can go slowly. We can look into the bracken."

"And into the river!" said Queenie half under her breath.

"Hats!" called Auntie Dot from the verandah. "You can't go out in all this heat without your hats on!"

But Queenie and Sophie were already away.

"We're following Pa!" Queenie shouted up to her as they ran off towards the Creek.

From all around the settlement now came the loud voices of men and boys as the search got under way.

"Coo-ee! Coo-ee! Coo-ee!"

The quiet forest rang with their cries.

"Coo-ee! Coo-ee!" called Sophie as she and Queenie set off along the tram-track into the bush.

"Bertie! Where are you?" called Queenie.

They moved slowly, poking into the bracken and ferns between the track and the river on their left and under the thick saplings on their right.

After about half a mile the track and the river began to draw apart. The tramway gradually climbed the side of the hill; the river kept to the bottom of the gully.

"Pa's been right up this track," said Queenie, pausing a minute between the rails. "P'raps we should stick to the river."

"The track's safer," said Sophie.

"Yes—but the river's really all right. I've often been fishing further up with Grandpa. Bertie's been there too."

Sophie wasn't happy to leave the solid tram-track behind her but Queenie seemed very sure of herself now. They struck off to the left towards the river and kept close to its edge. The water splashed and tumbled beside them. The tree-ferns grew thicker.

"Keep calling," said Queenie, moving a few yards away to the right. "Then we won't lose each other."

Sophie took up the cry again.

"Coo-ee! Coo-ee! Coo-ee!"

After each long call they both stood still and listened. No one answered. The bush was utterly quiet. Even the forest birds seemed strangely silent. All Sophie could hear was the distant cry of the other searchers for miles around.

"Queenie! Look!" she shrieked.

"What is it?"

Sophie was staring at a torn scrap of blue cloth, caught on the furry trunk of a tree-fern right by the water's edge.

"It's a bit of Bertie's shirt," she said.

"How do you know?" asked Queenie, coming closer to look.

"I did up his buttons for him. It's the same colour."

"Lots of people wear blue shirts," said Queenie.

"I'm sure it's his!" said Sophie.

"Let's keep moving," said Queenie.

The river ran under the bridge now with the tram-track high above their heads.

"Coo-ee!" called Queenie, pressing on beyond the bridge.

"He'd never come so far," Sophie muttered to herself, twisting the piece of blue cloth between her fingers and hanging back.

Something caught her eye. She bent down low to the ground.

"Oh!" she gasped. Her throat tightened.

On a patch of sticky mud by a clump of bracken was a child's footprint, each toe-mark firm and clear.

"Queenie! Come back! He must've come this way!"

Queenie ran and knelt beside her.

"No boots on!" she said. "There's snakes around here!"

Sophie couldn't help laughing in spite of her mounting fears.

"He didn't know he was going to get lost, Queenie," she said.

"Coo-ee!" called Queenie.

They listened hard.

From quite near at hand came the cry of a sad little voice.

"I'se vewy vewy tired."

"Bertie!" shrieked Queenie. "Where are you?"

"Here!" came the little voice again.

Where was it coming from? Sophie ran one way and Queenie the other. It was Sophie who found him.

Bertie lay curled up on the river bank under the long drooping fronds of a tree-fern, his arms around his knees. Black mud covered his bare feet and his hands. Even his face was smeared with mud and tears.

"I'se torn my nice new shirt, Soapy!" he said as he caught sight of her.

"Bertie!" cried Sophie. "We've found you!" She sprang forward and flung her arms around him.

Bertie began to cry.

"Queenie! He's here! He's not in the river!" called Sophie, struggling against strange tears herself.

Queenie ran up and threw herself on Bertie. She was overjoyed to see him. But in an instant her relief changed to sudden anger.

"Bertie! You're very naughty to wander off like that! Everyone's looking for you! Ma's very worried! And you haven't got your boots on, either!"

Bertie cried louder still. He bawled.

Sophie tried to pick him up. He was too heavy for her to carry for long, and she had to let him down again.

Queenie had recovered.

"We'll make a seat with our hands," she said. "That's the best way."

They grasped wrists and made a firm square seat for Bertie. He climbed on as they bent down and he slid one grubby arm round Queenie's neck and one round Sophie's.

"I'se vewy vewy hungwy!" he said.

Slowly the girls moved back along the river with their burden till they reached the tramway again. With aching arms they lowered him to the ground.

"We'll never carry him all the way," said Queenie. "I'll wait here with him and you run on to the mill. Tell Mr Greenbank. He'll come and get him. And tell Ma, too."

Queenie sat Bertie on one of the rails and took her place beside him. Sophie ran. The wooden sleepers seemed to fly under her feet.

"Mr Greenbank!" she called as soon as the grey mill and the little grey houses came into sight between the trees. "We've found him! Auntie Dot! Bertie's found!"

Mr Greenbank waved as he caught her message and hurried into the mill to sound the whistle once more. Four long blasts announced to the world that Bertie was safe. Auntie Dot came running down the steps of the house and hugged Sophie tight.

"Who found him?" she asked.

"I did," said Sophie.

Auntie Dot hugged her tighter still.

"It's lucky you came to the mill, Sophie," she said. "We just couldn't do without you."

Sophie smiled happily to herself, her face squashed hard against Auntie Dot's rough apron.

One by one, the searchers trailed back to the mill and to the hot cups of black tea in Auntie Dot's kitchen. Mr Greenbank carried Bertie home on his shoulders. Auntie Dot washed him all clean in the tin tub and gave him his tea. She tucked him up into Grandpa's bed though the sun was still beating down as bright and hot as ever.

"Soapy found me, Ma!" murmured Bertie as he drifted off to sleep, his little wooden engine safely under his pillow.

6. *Green Fern and Christmas Bush*

Slowly Christmas came closer. Most mornings Queenie and Sophie trudged out along the tram-track with Grandpa to watch the horses at work and to see the giant trees come down. It seemed to Sophie that Grandpa just couldn't keep away from those horses. He never interfered with Ray Sanders' way of doing things but he always hung about, leaning back against a tree trunk, while the horses strained and heaved at great logs along the gullies. He waited hopefully for the moment when Ray would sing out,

"Just lend a hand here, Harry, will you?"

The call always came. Whether Ray really needed Grandpa's help with the horses, Sophie wasn't ever quite sure. Perhaps he was just being kind. But Grandpa was ready at once, springing forward on his old legs to take hold of a bridle or to whisper into Clinker's ear or Bella's or to shout encouragement at the whole long team as they dragged another massive log to the landing platform or pulled the laden bogies back to the mill. Grandpa had a way with the horses all right. Sophie could see that. They seemed to respond to his hand and voice even better than to Ray's. Grandpa was their old friend and they'd worked together for years.

As the last log before dinner time was chained into place and the line of horses harnessed up for the run back to the mill, Sophie could choose whether she'd sooner be lifted up to ride on top of the log itself or to sit astride Clinker's wide back. Whichever she chose, it meant a scramble down and up again at the short tunnel so she wouldn't bump her head. She soon got used to that with Ray and Grandpa to help her and with Queenie scrambling down and up beside her. The log-ride felt much safer than the horse. The log was solid and it didn't move about beneath her. But the rough bark scratched her legs and there was only a rope or a chain to hold on to. She had to sit sideways with her legs dangling to left or right. Clinker's back was soft and warm and she could take a good firm grip of his heavy collar. But he swayed alarmingly as he plodded down the track and he snorted loudly from time to time and tossed his head. She could hear his noisy breathing and the sound of his great shoes striking hard against the wooden sleepers far down below. It took a few weeks before she felt more at ease perched up there on Clinker's back.

In the long hot afternoons when the logging crews were back at work in the forest again, the two girls wandered off with Bertie at their heels to explore the settlement. Bertie always dragged his wooden train behind him on a long piece of string.

"My puff-puff, Soapy," he explained to Sophie the first time they set off together.

"It's a train, Bertie," she said rather primly, "or an engine."

"No," said Queenie, "it's a loco, really. That's what Pa always calls it, anyway. But Bertie just says 'puff-puff '. He's only little, Sophie. Ma doesn't want him to grow up too fast. He's the last one."

"I hope my little brother or sister will be the last one!" Sophie's voice sounded almost fierce.

"Don't you want a little sister or brother?" asked Queenie in surprise.

Sophie shook her head.

"Mother and I get on all right—just the two of us together. When there's another one she won't have so much time for me. And it'll stay at home with her every day when I have to go to school. But perhaps it'll die. New babies do die sometimes. Mrs Dunphy told me that. Hers all died."

Queenie was silent.

"What's die?" shouted Bertie from behind them, straddling his little loco.

"Shh!" said Queenie sharply. "Bertie, let's race up the hill! Come on, Sophie!" and Queenie bounded away up the steep path between the houses, behind the vegetable gardens and the furthest back fences to the point at the top of the ridge where the clearing ended and the grey-green bush began again.

The top of that ridge was the place that Sophie liked best in the whole little township of Stringybark Mill. She climbed up there most afternoons with Queenie and Bertie and she climbed up there alone in the early evenings after the whistle had blown and the mill had stopped its racket for the day. She liked to sit on a warm log where lizards darted over the bark and look down at the houses and the river below. The spiny anteaters that the mill children called porcupines sometimes crept out of the bush behind her and snuffled about among the dry gum nuts on the ground. Quiet wallabies stood poised between the trees, watching her warily as she watched them. Cockatoos and lorikeets squawked and fluttered above her in the trees and a friendly kookaburra swooped down to snatch up a lizard. Sophie sat on till she heard Auntie Dot calling to her from the verandah next to the forge.

"Sophie! Sophie! It's tea time. Come on down now!"

The heat of that summer mounted day after day. Sophie was amazed that the fallers and the loggers went on working through it all. It was a motionless heat with no lashing north wind to bring the fear of bush fires but no cool south breeze either at the end of the day to bring a few hours' relief. The nights were almost as bad as the days. Sophie and Queenie tossed about in their bed under the burning roof. Uncle Ted took his pillow out to the verandah and lay there on the bare floor-boards, regardless of the singing mosquitoes, rather than spend one more night inside the breathless house. Even the bright forest birds seemed to feel the terrible heat. They became uncannily silent as if they were too hot even to whistle out loud or to move their tired feathers. Only in the very early morning down by the cool of the river could they manage to carol and call.

The working horses needed water and still more water. Grandpa was on the job all day long, leading them down to the river and waiting while their great tongues lapped noisily and their front hoofs splashed about among the wet stones. He threw buckets of cold water over their sweating flanks and even over their drooping heads.

The mill saws and the cicadas screeched on and on together. The heat and the noise seemed to fuse into one inside Sophie's head. The milk brought from Forrest turned sour in the cans. The meat, carefully hung in a wire cage from a tree in every back yard, went off. The butter and the dripping melted even inside the coolgardie safes with their strips of wet cloth hanging down around them. Auntie Dot's kitchen was like a furnace. The little fire-stove roared away. Auntie Dot kept out of it as much as she could but meals had to be cooked, heat or no heat, good meat or bad. And on Monday afternoons, when Sophie helped her peg out the washing, the sheets at the start of the line were bone dry by the time she'd reached the other end.

"There's a cool change coming, me darling!" Uncle Ted would say cheerfully every morning, going out to the verandah and holding up one wet finger to catch some imaginary breeze. "I can smell it in the air, Dot! Straight off the sea it's blowing, straight off the sea!" But every evening he had to admit that he'd been wrong.

"Tomorrow, me darling!" he'd say to Auntie Dot at tea time. "This can't go on forever."

But it seemed to Sophie that it would go on forever.

Mother's letter came without fail every week — one special page for her inside the letter to Grandpa. The handwriting ran both ways on both sides of the sheet, the lines crossing over each other in bewildering confusion. Sophie puzzled over the spidery words for hours. Drought was Mother's main topic. Drought was burning the farm to dust. Sophie could imagine the thick silences at meal times as Dad brooded over his dry-baked paddocks. Mother never mentioned the coming baby. Sophie began to hope that she'd changed her mind about the whole thing. Perhaps they needn't have the baby after all.

"And what do you do for Christmas up at the farm, me darling?" asked Uncle Ted one tea-time as Sophie folded up her letter and put it away.

"We don't do much. Dad kills a chook. Mum plucks it and stuffs it with thyme and breadcrumbs and butter. And I hang up a stocking and Santa Claus comes — only it's not really Santa Claus, you know, it's just . . . "

"Sh!" burst in Queenie and Auntie Dot with one breath. They looked anxiously towards Lottie and Effie and Bertie in case they'd heard, but they were all too busy eating.

"And your Dad has a few drinks with his mates, I daresay. In at Birregurra. Nice little pub there," said Uncle Ted.

"No, no. Nothing like that. He hasn't got any mates. And anyway, he doesn't drink. Mother says we're lucky. We don't have any trouble with him that way."

"I dwink!" shouted Bertie, swallowing down his sour milk

in huge gulps and grinning at Sophie over the top of his glass.

"But don't you decorate the house at Christmas? With green stuff and paper streamers?" asked Queenie.

Sophie shook her head.

"But you do go to church, dear, don't you?" said Auntie Dot.

"No. We never go. It's too far to Birregurra. Anyway, Dad works on Christmas Day. He says it's no different from any other day. Except for the chook. We do have the chook."

Uncle Ted chuckled into his beard.

"Well, Sophie me darling, you're in for a surprise or two, I reckon. Christmas down here at the mill is a real Christmas. Just you wait and see! You'll have something to tell your poor mother about when you get back to the farm. Won't she, Dot?"

Auntie Dot smiled but Sophie thought she looked a bit worried too.

"Remember what you promised last year, Ted," she said.

"Promised, me darling? Did I ever promise you a thing about Christmas? I don't remember it at all!"

"Ted, you know very well you did!"

Uncle Ted laughed and pushed back his chair from the table.

"We don't work here on Christmas Day, Sophie me darling. That's one thing you can be sure of."

"You don't work on Boxing Day either, Pa!" said Queenie. "You couldn't! It's just as well the boss gives you all a couple of weeks off!"

"Sh!" said Auntie Dot as she began to clear away the dishes more noisily than usual. "That's enough, Queenie. This Christmas is going to be different. A promise is a promise."

Three days before Christmas, Queenie and Sophie went shopping for presents in the little general store near the mill. Uncle Ted had given them each a whole shilling to spend. Sophie had never held so much in her hand before and had certainly never been faced with the task of buying seven presents. She had a happy hour with Queenie going carefully along the back shelves in the store. Mr Johnson let them take their time. He hung a kerosene lamp in the darkest corner so the girls could see better into all his jars and boxes. Sophie was pleased with her shopping. A plug of tobacco for Grandpa, a box of yellow matches for Uncle

Ted, a packet of shining hair pins for Auntie Dot, a green hair ribbon for Queenie, a sheet of flower transfers for Lottie, a tiny doll's teacup for Effie and a long black liquorice strap for Bertie. Back at the house Auntie Dot pulled open a drawer stuffed with smooth white tissue paper. Sophie took seven sheets of the paper and a ball of string. Alone on the bed she wrapped each present in turn and wrote the name on each one so she wouldn't get them all mixed up. One little bundle looked so much like the other.

"Will I hang up my stocking on Christmas Eve?" she asked Auntie Dot that same afternoon.

"Of course you will, dear! Santa always comes to the mill. He knows you're here. He won't forget you."

"But Auntie," said Sophie, dropping her voice, "don't you know it's really only . . . "

"Just you wait and see," said Auntie Dot, smiling at her.

The more Sophie looked at Auntie Dot the more she saw she was not really so like Mother at all. They did have same dark hair coiled back in a heavy bun with a brown net to hold it in place, and their hands were broad with short strong fingers, but where Mother's face was all creased and lined and her skin baked brown from her years at the farm and the set of her mouth very straight, almost hard, Auntie Dot was altogether softer and pinker and more smiling. Mother didn't smile much.

But though the two faces were so different, the two voices were exactly the same. Often Sophie caught her breath in surprise when Auntie Dot called her from behind. For an instant she imagined that Mother had come to the mill to take her back home again but when she turned round there was Auntie's pink smiling face. She felt a stab of disappointment every time but also a surge of relief. She didn't want to go home just yet. Not till after Christmas anyway.

On Christmas Eve the logging crew didn't go out to bring home any logs. The fallers didn't cut down any trees. But all the men were out along the gullies as usual with their axes and saws. All the horses were out there too with the timber trucks rolling along behind them.

"Come on, Sophie," said Grandpa. "You too, Queenie. We don't want all the mill kids on this job but you two can help."

He hurried them off along the tram-track till they caught up with the horses on a high ridge above Coldwater Creek. Sophie had never seen all twenty horses out in the bush together. They were lined up now between the rails and facing the way home to the mill. They stood quietly, hardly even moving a hoof, their tails flicking lazily at the flies. Sophie's eyes travelled down the long row searching for Clinker. Black horses, brown horses, grey, white and piebald. Eighty heavy feathered fetlocks. There was Clinker! The fourth from the far end. Sophie wandered down alone towards him.

"Clinker!" she called out softly.

Slowly Clinker turned his head. Sophie could see the white splash between his blinkered eyes. He was looking straight at her, nodding his big head up and down, up and down. He whinnied loudly. He knew her all right. She moved closer still and put one hand against his thick hot coat. She kept her eyes anxiously on his feet. She edged away again. Down at the end of the line stood the four empty timber bogies, one behind the other. Sophie walked back to Grandpa.

"I'll stay here with the horses," he said. "You two can slide down into the gully. Be careful now."

From far below where the creek ran fast between stones came the sounds of laughing and splashing.

"Come on!" said Queenie.

She sat herself promptly on the gully's edge and began to slip and slide over bracken and grass towards the bottom. Sophie hesitated for a minute but then cautiously slid down behind her, clutching at low bushes to break her speed, steering round sharp rocks and saplings, digging her fingers into the moss. Down by the creek the men were cutting green fronds from the tall tree-ferns and skylarking about, flicking water at each other from the dripping leaves. They ran from one fern to the next, taking one frond here, another there, so none was stripped too bare. The long fronds were bundled together and tied with rope. The men passed the bundles from hand to hand up the slope to the tram-track and piled them on to the bogies.

"What's it for?" asked Sophie.

"Christmas decorations. We put those branches all along the

front verandahs. We turn the billiard shed into a kind of forest. You'll see. Let's get some maidenhair fern now. There's lots along the creek here."

Sophie and Queenie gathered armfuls of the delicate fern that trailed in the water and clung to the rocks. Their cotton dresses were soaked through by the time they had staggered up the gully's side again to the tramline with their dripping load.

"Good lasses!" called Ray Sanders who was helping the fallers to stack the bogies high with the great fern fronds. "Bring it over here. There's still room on this one."

Queenie darted off again as soon as she'd handed over her bundle of maidenhair.

"Come on, Sophie. This way. There's one more thing we always find. I know a special place. Come on!"

Sophie ran behind her. Queenie didn't dive down into the gully again but went straight ahead along the tram-track, deeper still into the bush. She left the track and climbed the densely wooded hillside. How she knew which turn to take, which trees to pass and where to stop at last, Sophie didn't know. She simply panted along behind, her wet dress drying off quickly in the heat, her scratched legs stinging.

"Here we are!" cried Queenie as she dashed straight into a shady clump of blue-gum saplings. "I knew I'd find the place."

Sophie followed. Then she stopped suddenly in her tracks and drew in her breath in surprise. She'd never seen anything like it. Beyond the blue-gums was a patch of shining green bushes, their branches heavy with white scented flowers, every petal flecked with lilac.

"Christmas bush!" shouted Queenie triumphantly. "We can pick as much as we like."

Sophie wasn't sure that she wanted to pick the flowers at all. They looked so still and perfect just as they were on the bushes. But Queenie was leaping ahead of her and beginning to gather in the trailing stems with their long cascades of flowers. Sophie worked more slowly, sniffing at the blazing white bushes as she went. Their arms were soon full and still the patch of Christmas bush seemed untouched.

"Queenie! Sophie! Hurry up there! We're going back to the

mill!" Grandpa's voice, thin but clear, rang out through the bush.

"Coming!" called Queenie back again and the two of them ran down the hill and along the track to the bogies piled high with greenery.

"Christmas bush!" she shouted to Grandpa.

"Well done!" said Grandpa. "Now both of you come and sit up here. Hold on tight to those flowers of yours."

He was looking down at them from the top of a load of tree-ferns. Ray Sanders lifted Queenie up and then Sophie. They sank into the springy nest of fern. Ray walked right along the string of horses to Bella at the head of the team.

"Off we go!" he called with his hand on Bella's bridle. "That's the way, Bella! Get along there, Sandy! Up we come, Diamond, up we come!"

Ray called out to each of the horses by name. Their load was ridiculously easy today. No heavy tree trunks to lug back along the track. One horse could have pulled the lot but Ray liked all his horses to be there on Christmas Eve. As the four bogies started to roll, the men scrambled on board and sat in the middle of the branches. Grandpa began to sing from the top of the first truck, his reedy voice carrying right back to the fallers at the end and right up over the nodding heads of twenty horses to Ray Sanders out in front of the green cavalcade. It was a song Sophie had never heard before though Queenie was humming the tune to herself.

The holly and the ivy
When they are both full grown,
Of all the trees that are in the wood,
The holly bears the crown.

"But it's not holly," murmured Sophie, clinging on tight to her sweet-smelling Christmas bush and rocking about in her bed of fern. "And it's not ivy either."

"I know that," Queenie whispered back to her, "but it's just some old song of Grandpa's. He sings it every Christmas when we go back to the mill with the fern. He says he used to sing it in England when he was a boy. They've got plenty of holly over there, he says. Ivy too, probably."

"I bet they haven't got Christmas bush," said Sophie, burying her face in the white flowers. "Poor things!"

At Stringybark Mill all the women and children were waiting for them by the landing platform. The whistle blew one long piercing shriek and a great excited shout went up as Bella plodded into the township with all the other horses strung out behind her. When the trucks themselves rolled into sight with the men waving and calling from up on the piles of green fronds and Queenie and Sophie almost buried under their bundles of Christmas bush, the shouting grew louder and wilder. Everyone ran forward to help with the unloading. Every family grabbed armfuls of fern. In half an hour every little verandah was heavy with the stuff. It was hanging down from the gutters on the roof, it was woven through the handrails by the steps, it was draped around the windows, it was propped in the corners near the ferrets' cages. Then the stables, the bake-house, the butcher's shed and the general store were swathed in fern. The drab little grey township was green.

"Now for the billiard shed," said Queenie, picking up her bunch of Christmas bush again and running to the shed's open door.

The billiard shed had been transformed. The women were still hard at work inside, sweeping the dirt floor, re-hanging the faded washed curtains at the windows, pushing the green baize table to the farthest end and covering it with a long white sheet. They had hammered up the branches of tree-fern along every wall till the bare boards were hidden by the leaves. There were even some fronds hanging from the ceiling above but how they'd got right up there Sophie couldn't imagine.

The women had finished. The billiard shed was a cool cavern of fern. The stale smell of tobacco had gone and the whole place smelled clean and fresh like the mossy banks of Coldwater Creek. Queenie and Sophie arranged their Christmas bush in a row of four large jam jars that stood ready and waiting on the sheet-covered table.

Queenie went to the door and looked back inside the shed with a smile of immense satisfaction on her face.

"There we are!" she cried triumphantly. "Now we're all ready for Christmas at the mill!"

7. *The Strangest Christmas*

Sophie was getting rather tired of being told to "Wait and see" every time she asked about Christmas. She wished she knew just what to expect. Everyone else at the mill seemed to know exactly what the next step would be. They'd all been through it every year for years on end and she could see that they loved to do things just as they'd always done them before. But for Sophie every moment was strange and new.

"What's next?" she wondered to herself as she and Queenie walked back up the hill from the billiard shed for tea. She was dead tired. Her thighs ached from the bumpy slide down to the creek and her arms ached from the bundles of fern and flowers she'd carried.

"You two do look a mess!" laughed Auntie Dot when she saw them coming through the door.

Queenie and Sophie gazed at each other in surprise. Then they couldn't help laughing themselves. Their faces were smeared with dust and mud. Their cotton dresses were torn and stained with green. Their boots were scuffed. Sophie's plaits had come undone so her hair flopped down over her eyes. Queenie's red hair was full of leaves and white petals.

"A bath first," said Auntie Dot firmly. "I'll bring the tub into the living room. There's no room for it in the kitchen tonight. I'm far too busy and all the little ones are helping me and getting in the way."

She carried in the big oval tin bath from its hook just outside the back door and set it down in the centre of the square of brown linoleum in the main room of the house. She pushed the armchairs well back out of the way and brought in two kettlefuls of boiling water, one in each hand, and poured them into the tub.

"Don't get in yet. I've got to add the cold."

She came back with a bucket of cold water and tipped it in. She knelt down and tested the temperature with her bare elbow.

"That's just right now girls," she said. "You can both get in together but no splashing. This room's nice and clean for

Christmas. I don't want to have to do it all over again."

Queenie and Sophie stripped off their dirty clothes and stepped into the warm water. By crouching with knees to chin they could both just fit into the bath, one each end and facing each other. There was hardly a crack of room for the cake of yellow soap or the white flannel.

"You wash first," offered Queenie, "and I'll just sit. Then I'll wash. If we both move at the same time we'll only slosh water all over Ma's precious floor."

Cautiously Sophie manoeuvred the soap and the flannel around in the tub and managed to wash herself from face to foot. Then Queenie did the same.

"Ma!" bellowed Queenie towards the kitchen door. "What about our hair? We can't have it filthy for Christmas!"

Auntie Dot came back into the room with flour on her hands.

"What a moment to pick, Queenie! I'm just mixing the pudding for tomorrow. But you're right. Those heads of yours do need a wash. Get them good and wet while I wipe this flour off my hands. Lottie can stir the pudding."

Sophie and Queenie passed the dripping flannel back and forth from one hand to the other, soaking their hair till the water ran down their faces. When Auntie Dot set to work with the hard soap, Sophie squealed out loud in surprise. Auntie's hands were strong. She lathered up first the dark head and then the red one. She rubbed and scrubbed vigorously with those iron fingers of hers and took not the slightest notice of wild shrieks as the soap went into Queenie's eyes or as Sophie tried to squirm away from under her grip.

"You're cruel, Ma!" shouted Queenie, half laughing and half crying, her head bent down close to the water. "That's what you are! Cruel!"

"Wait till we get to the rinsing, my girl," said Auntie Dot. "Then you'll really have something to shriek about."

"Not outside, Ma! Everyone will see us!"

"Not a soul will see you, Queenie. They're all far too busy. They'll hear you, no doubt, but that doesn't matter a jot. I'm not having water slopped all over this room on Christmas Eve. Come on. Out into the back yard with the two of you."

Sophie climbed from the tub and followed Queenie, naked and dripping, through to the kitchen and out of the back door. A trail of wet footprints ran after them. They stood with twigs and broken gum-nuts crunching under their feet and they bent down obediently towards the dry grass while Auntie Dot poured bucketful after bucketful of cold water over their soapy heads. Queenie bellowed and Sophie sobbed. Auntie Dot marched relentlessly back to the big green tank by the back door for yet one more chilly bucketful.

"A pair of cry-babies, that's what you are! Dear little Bertie never makes all that noise. Lottie and Effie are angels. I rinsed all their heads out here this afternoon and not a peep from any of them. Goodness knows what the neighbours will think."

"They'll think you're murdering us!" shouted Queenie. "And you are!"

Suddenly the rinsing had stopped. Auntie Dot ran her hands through Sophie's hair and then through Queenie's to hear it squeak.

"There we are! Clean for Christmas! Now wait here while I bring out your towels."

Sophie straightened up. She and Queenie looked at each other and laughed. It was all over. Auntie Dot wrapped a white towel round Queenie and another round Sophie.

"Get dry and dressed now," she said, turning back to her pudding in the kitchen. "Mr Plant is coming for tea, remember."

Queenie groaned.

"Not Mr Plant, Ma!" she said, following her mother inside. "We had him for tea last year. It must be Mrs Roberts' turn to have him."

"That's true enough, Queenie. But Mrs Roberts is busy with her new baby. You know that. So I said we'd have him again."

"Ma!" moaned Queenie and trailed off to the bedroom with Sophie behind her.

"Who's this Mr Plant?" Sophie asked as they pulled on their clean clothes.

Queenie groaned. "He's not so bad down in the billiard shed but I hate him coming to tea."

He was there already, seated at the table, when Queenie and

Sophie came into the room half an hour later, their clean hair dry and brushed smooth. He was a small man in a tight black suit and a narrow black cravat at his throat. He wore round tortoise-shell glasses that caught the light from the window. Sophie couldn't see his eyes beneath them.

"Won't you take your coat off, Mr Plant?" Auntie Dot was saying. "You've had a long ride out here to the mill. You must be hot."

"No thank you, Mrs Blakeley. I don't want to catch a chill, you know. Just another glass of water, if you please. Most refreshing."

His voice was surprisingly deep and loud.

Auntie Dot poured him the water from her best glass jug.

"Is he the minister?" whispered Sophie to Queenie, eyeing his black suit as they walked round the table to their proper places.

"No. He's just a preacher," Queenie whispered back. "Works in the bank in Forrest. Preaches on Sundays."

Auntie Dot frowned at Queenie to stop her whispering.

"And this," she said, putting one firm hand on Sophie's shoulder, "this is my sister's child from up at the farm. She's staying with us till after Christmas. Sophie Ramsdale."

Mr Plant beamed at Sophie. His spectacles glinted.

"He looks all right," thought Sophie to herself. "I can't see what Queenie's making so much fuss about."

Uncle Ted came in looking spruce and cheerful. He shook Mr Plant by the hand and took his usual place.

"Now, Mr Plant," said Auntie Dot, "would you say grace for us before we eat?"

This surprised Sophie. Auntie Dot didn't normally bother about grace.

"Delighted!" said Mr Plant and bowed his head. All the other eight heads were bowed too. Sophie turned slightly sideways in her chair and half opened her eyes so she could get a better look at Mr Plant. She could see in behind his spectacles. His eyes were tightly shut. He pulled hard on the cravat and tilted up his chin again. He took a deep breath.

"O Lord!" he began, lifting both hands off the tablecloth for an instant and then putting them down again. His voice was pitched several tones higher and he seemed almost to sing his words rather than say them. The prayer was slow and melancholy. Sophie shivered though she wasn't cold.

"O Lord!" Mr Plant repeated. "We thank Thee that Thou hast gathered us together around this simple board at the blessed season of our dear Saviour's birth so long ago in Bethlehem. We are not worthy to gather up the crumbs from under Thy table. Thou knowest the blackness of our hearts. Wash us, O Lord, as white as snow in the blood of the Lamb! Let us ever hold fast," (and here Sophie thought Mr Plant was turning his head slightly to the left and addressing his remarks to Uncle Ted) "let us ever hold fast to that precious gift of *temperance*. Help us to resist the wiles of the Evil One. Let nothing come to spoil the peace of this blessed season of our dear Saviour's birth so far away in Bethlehem. In His name and for His sake we ask it, O Lord. Amen."

Sophie peered under the table to see what crumbs Mr Plant had been talking about but Auntie's floor was as spotless as ever. And who was the Evil One? She looked around at every smiling face. It can't be anyone here, she thought.

Uncle Ted was grinning broadly. Once again he shook Mr Plant vigorously by the hand.

"Thank you, Mr Plant, thank you. You do a good job at those prayers. A very merry Christmas to you!"

Mr Plant looked pleased. He rubbed his hands together as Auntie Dot carried in all the food. He tucked his white napkin high up under his chin and spread it carefully over his chest. Everyone began to eat. Thick slices of cold mutton. Hot mashed potatoes. Yellow pickles and green beans.

"Is my heart black?" asked Effie with interest, her mouth stuffed full of potato.

"Yes, my little one," said Mr Plant breezily, "black as coal. But have no fear. The Saviour is nigh." And he reached across the table to help himself to another spoonful of yellow pickles.

"Sh, Effie," said Auntie Dot, looking rather worried. "I'll explain it to you later."

Bertie's eyes opened wide. He put down his spoon and began to rub the spot where he thought his black heart must be.

Queenie giggled.

"Eat up, Bertie," said Auntie Dot sharply.

Luckily Lottie changed the subject. She was wriggling with excitement.

"Have you brought the magic lantern, Mr Plant?" she asked. "And the squeeze-box too? Just like last year?"

Mr Plant nodded and smiled.

"Just like last year," he said, "just like last year."

"In the saddle-bags?" asked Effie.

"In the saddle-bags. Just like last year. One each side of Tilly's saddle. I had to have those bags specially made, you know. Can't buy things like that in any old shop. Specially made for me by a man in Colac. Did it for nothing too. An offering to the Lord."

There was a pause while Mr Plant chewed his next mouthful carefully.

"Did you ride a horse here?" asked Sophie, trying to imagine Mr Plant up on a horse's back. "The whole way down the tram-track?"

"Yes, my little one. That's not far, you know. Only six miles. Every Sunday I ride further than that. Taking the pure milk of the gospel to those poor souls who hunger and thirst after righteousness." He held out his plate for another slice of meat.

Sophie wondered who the poor souls were and where they lived but before she could ask her question Grandpa was speaking.

"I gave your old Tilly a good feed of oats, Mr Plant," he said. "She'll be right as rain down there in the stables with Bella and Diamond and Clinker and all the others. New company'll do them good. You want to be careful going back along that tramway in the dark, you know. Fallen logs. Can't see them in the dark. Came a cropper there myself one night." And Grandpa was off on one of his long stories about the past. That story led to another as it generally did. Mr Plant couldn't get another word in for ten minutes or more. At last Grandpa paused for breath and Mr Plant rushed quickly into the gap, turning face-on to Uncle Ted.

"We'll be seeing you down in the billiard shed tonight I hope, Mr Blakeley. It's not just for the ladies and kiddies, you know. *All* are welcome. Young and old." He beamed at Uncle Ted.

"We'll both be there, won't we Ted," said Auntie Dot before

Uncle had time to open his mouth. "Most of the men are coming. It gets Christmas off to a good start, I always say."

The meal was over. The teapot was empty.

"Will I just offer another little prayer, Mrs Blakeley?" asked Mr Plant eagerly.

"No, fanks!" said Bertie, scrambling off his chair.

"Yes, please, Mr Plant," said Auntie Dot, pulling Bertie back again.

Sophie didn't listen this time and she didn't bother to watch the preacher's face. His voice rose and fell, loud and sad as before. Black hearts were certainly mentioned once again but Sophie was thinking about the two big saddle-bags, specially made in Colac, and the magic lantern and the squeeze-box. When would she see them and what were they for?

By the time Uncle Ted and his family arrived at the billiard shed with Mr Plant, every man, woman and child from the mill township seemed to be already packed inside. The women sat stiffly in their best dresses on the chairs down each side wall. The children crouched or squatted on the floor in front. The men stood at the back just inside the door, leaning against the fern fronds that hung on the wall, laughing and talking loudly together with their arms folded across their chests.

An excited buzz ran through the waiting crowd when Mr Plant appeared at last.

"Make way for the preacher there!" shouted someone.

The men and the children edged back a few feet to clear a space for Mr Plant in the very centre of the shed. Uncle Ted had put the saddle-bags gently onto the floor and Mr Plant began to undo the buckles. He set up his heavy magic lantern on a metal stand that almost unfolded itself from the bag and he arranged a neat pile of square glass plates beside the lantern. Mr Greenbank himself climbed up on the flower-filled billiard table and, stepping carefully around the jam-jars, he hung up a white sheet from the ceiling to serve as a screen. All the curtains were drawn across the open windows to block out the evening light. The door was shut. It was pitch dark inside the shed now and unbearably stuffy and hot.

Mr Plant wasted no time. He had lit a little flame inside his lantern. The strange fumes set everyone coughing. Then he slid his first glass plate into its grooves in front of the light and a brown flickering picture began to appear on the hanging sheet. The coughing stopped at once.

"There we are!" said Mr Plant.

"What is it?" whispered Sophie to Queenie as she gazed puzzled at the brown blotches on the screen.

"It's a picture show with magic pictures!" said Queenie full of confidence. "That's Bethlehem there."

"How do you know?"

"He told us last year. You can see the houses if you look hard enough."

Sophie wasn't at all sure that she could see any houses. She looked again. Then, suddenly, in the flickering brown shadows she began to see them. Flat-roofed and square with ragged palm trees drooping beside them and women in long-flowing garments with water-pots balanced on their heads.

"And so, my dear friends," said Mr Plant, swaying back on his heels and lapsing into the sad, sing-song voice again, "and so we come once again to this blessed season of Christmas. How happy I am to be amongst you once more and to lead your thoughts to that far-away country of Palestine."

Sophie thought he didn't sound so very happy.

"Here we have the little houses of Bethlehem just as they were two thousand years ago and here . . . " (he slid the first plate out and the second plate in) ". . . here we have the lovely spring flowers by the sea of Galilee."

The next picture slid into view.

"The Garden of Gesthemane," announced Mr Plant.

"What's that got to do with Christmas?" whispered Sophie.

"Nothing," whispered Queenie. "He just shows all his pictures."

"Has he ever been there? To Palestine?"

"Never been further than Colac."

The crowd in the billiard shed were not at all worried that the pictures jumped about from one part of Palestine to another. They gazed silent and fascinated as one magic image followed the next in quick succession. Mr Plant certainly knew what all the places were. He knew Palestine like the back of his hand. Jerusalem and

Jericho, hills and valleys, narrow streets and thick stone walls, sheep and shepherds — all in the same faded brown with the same bulges where the sheet bulged and the same strange quivering light that flashed out from the acrid lantern.

Sophie stared in amazement at another world unfolding in front of her eyes. She hardly even heard Mr Plant's sad voice droning on. He reached the end of his pile of picture plates and then, for good measure, showed them all again in reverse order till Bethlehem's houses came into view again.

"And now for our Christmas carols," he said more brightly.

Bethlehem slid swiftly out of sight and in its place came the large printed words of Good King Wenceslas. Mr Plant bent down in the dark to feel for his accordion and with a couple of loud opening chords he launched straight in, leading the singing himself through verse after verse.

The heat in the billiard shed was stifling. Sophie could feel her damp dress sticking unpleasantly to her back. She shifted around on the hard floor, trying to get more comfortable, wriggling an inch or two further from the warmth of Queenie's body on one side and Bertie's on the other. The people were all singing lustily, their feet tapping in time with the music, one old familiar carol succeeding another as Mr Plant slid the words in and out of his lantern and changed to a new set of chords.

Sophie herself didn't know all the carols and hymns but everyone else seemed to know them. Ice and snow. Frost and sleet. It must be a funny place over there, she thought to herself. Nothing like Stringybark Mill!

The last song was a quiet one. Behind the English words Sophie could just catch Mrs Schwartz from the bake-house singing some foreign-sounding hymn of her own. But the tune was the same.

Silent night, holy night,
All is calm, all is bright,
Round yon virgin, mother and child,
Holy infant so tender and mild,
Sleep in heavenly peace
Sleep in heavenly peace.

There was a moment's silence in the shed. Then Mr Plant cleared his throat. Sophie guessed he was going to pray again. Queenie nudged her. But before he had a chance to launch into his prayer, Mr Greenbank was on his feet in the dark.

"Thank you, Mr Plant, thank you. And a very happy Christmas from all of us here at the mill. Let's have some light there. I can't see a thing."

Someone pushed open the door and the women pulled back the curtains from the windows. A couple of lamps were brought in and held high over the crowd. Mr Greenbank gave Mr Plant his present in an envelope.

"And a very merry Christmas to you all," said Mr Greenbank.

A cheer went up and the people began to surge towards the door.

"Don't knock over my lantern!" cried Mr Plant, holding on to it with both hands. The accordion was wedged between his feet.

The pale evening light had flooded back into the billiard shed. The crowd had gone. Mr Plant packed up his saddle-bags and went off to the stables with Grandpa to collect his horse.

Sophie and Queenie watched as Mr Greenbank climbed up on the table again to pull down the sheet screen.

"The wife and I are off to Forrest in the morning," he said. "Our married daughter's having the whole family for Christmas. We'll be back on Boxing Day. Tell your Pa, will you, Queenie?"

Queenie nodded.

"Happy Christmas, Mr Greenbank," she said.

"And the same to you."

The sheet was down and rolled up. Mr Greenbank jumped from the table and set off home. Queenie and Sophie were the only ones left in the shed.

"Let's just straighten up our flowers," said Queenie. "Mr Greenbank's pushed them all around."

Sophie helped her to re-arrange the row of jam jars with their heavy sweet cascades of Christmas bush along the billiard table.

"What's that?" asked Sophie, her foot knocking against something hard.

She lifted the long white tablecloth to one side and peered underneath. Two blackwood barrels were stowed there, side by side, their silver taps gleaming in the yellow light from the last lamp.

"That's just the beer," said Queenie placidly. "Mr Greenbank always has a good few gallons sent down for Christmas Day. The men all like to have a drink or two after the dinner. Come on, Sophie. We're going to hang up our stockings. Santa's coming—and he knows you're here!"

Bertie, in his nightshirt, was setting out milk and biscuits for Santa Claus on the verandah. Effie and Lottie were watching him.

"Santa can't get down our chimney," Queenie explained seriously to Sophie. "It's too small. So he just comes through the front door like anyone else. We leave it propped wide open for him, don't we, Bertie?"

Bertie laid a small bundle of hay beside the biscuits.

"That's for the reindeer," said Effie.

"Do reindeer eat hay?" asked Sophie, surprised.

"Of course they do!" said Queenie. "They're just like our horses at the mill. They pull his sleigh all round the world."

The five stockings were hung at the end of the beds. A hot breathless night closed in on the township and the mill. Sophie slept.

There was no whistle on Christmas morning but Bertie woke everyone far too early with his shrieks of delight. His stocking was crammed to the brim. He ran to the verandah with Sophie close behind him to make sure that Santa had managed to find his provisions in the dark. Sure enough the hay and the biscuits had completely vanished, apart from a few stray wisps and a scattering of crumbs. The tall glass was empty but still stained with milk.

"He's been! He's been!" shouted Bertie happily and ran back to unpack his stocking all over the bed. Grandpa groaned and rolled over, his face to the wall.

Sophie herself had never had such a stocking on Christmas Day as the one that hung bulging beside Queenie's from the rail at the foot of the iron bed. At home Mother had always made sure she had something nice. A couple of new white collars, perhaps, or a set of handkerchiefs, a few wrapped lollies and a book. Always a book. But this stocking was absolutely stuffed. Sophie pulled the things out one by one. First came a gingham apron all cross-stitched in green thread. Then a tiny naked china doll.

A skein of blue wool and a pair of bone needles. A red wooden top and a whip to set it spinning on the floor. A string of white beads. A bag of clear cold marbles with colours whirling inside them. A cone of paper full of Liquorice All-Sorts and an orange right down in the toe. Propped beside the stocking was a flat square parcel that was too big to fit inside. Sophie tore off the brown paper. A book! Mother hadn't forgotten. Or Santa. Whoever it was.

Sophie climbed back into bed and pulled up the sheet. She put a Liquorice All-Sort into her mouth and began to read at once. All around her, Queenie, Lottie and Effie were exclaiming over the treasure-trove that tumbled from their stockings. Christmas had begun.

After breakfast was over, Sophie wandered down to the stables alone. Queenie was helping Auntie Dot to stuff the two plump rabbits and to boil the pudding for dinner. Grandpa had already watered and fed the twenty horses this morning. Ray Sanders was up in Colac for Christmas and Grandpa was in charge of the horses again. There was nothing he liked better. Sophie had expected to find him still in the stables but when she looked in at the open door there was no sign of him. He was probably back at the house, stacking some firewood in the yard or polishing up old bits of harness.

Her old fears did not grip her now. She could stand there looking in at the two long rows of horses in their stalls without any sick wave of panic rising inside her. But still she felt cautious about going right inside. Just standing at the door was enough. She could pick out Clinker perfectly well from there—the third stall down on the left-hand side.

Sophie stiffened. There was something odd about the horses today. They seemed restless and excited. Ears were pricked and tails were lashing. Bella kicked out suddenly at the boards of her stall. Diamond neighed loudly—not his usual comfortable neigh but a cry that was tense with fear. Sophie was puzzled.

"What on earth's the matter with you all?" she called out to them from the doorway.

Clinker reared up suddenly and snorted wildly. Sophie had to go in now. Only a few paces to his stall. She looked over the barrier and down at Clinker's four great feathered feet. They pawed angrily at the straw. She looked further in towards his massive dark shoulders and head.

"Clinker! What is it?" she said.

His head jerked round towards her from the far end of the stall. Then she saw it and screamed. A glinting copperhead snake was hanging fast to Clinker's muzzle. Its fangs had gripped him on the soft flesh just above his nostrils. The nostrils gaped wide in pain and terror.

Sophie ran. Out of the stables into the hot sunshine again, past the mill, up the slope to the blacksmith's shop and on to the house next door.

"Grandpa!" she called, her voice choking in her throat. "Where are you?"

She pounded up the steps to the verandah.

"Grandpa!" she called again. "There's a snake biting Clinker! It's hanging on to his nose. Quick! Quick! Come quick!"

Grandpa heard her. Just about the whole township heard her. He came running round from the back of the house, snatching up the snake-stick that always stood ready against the wall as he ran. Uncle Ted burst out of the front door at the same instant. Sophie turned and ran with them, back down the hill to the stables.

Grandpa was the first to get there. Uncle Ted and Sophie were close behind him. The snake had gone. Clinker's head drooped low and the other horses shuffled their feet noisily.

"Find that damned snake, Ted," snapped Grandpa angrily, throwing him the snake-stick. "We've got to know what it is."

Uncle Ted moved quickly from stall to stall, pushing the straw about, poking into the mangers, speaking quietly to soothe the frightened horses. He kept well clear of their hoofs. No snake.

Then Sophie caught a brief glimpse of a flickering tail just as it disappeared under a loose board at the other end of the stables.

"There it goes, Uncle!" she cried out. "Look! Through the back wall! Quick!"

Uncle Ted dashed out of the door and round to the back by the river. Sophie didn't follow. She could hear his stick crashing down relentlessly on the snake's writhing back. She didn't want to watch. She turned to find Grandpa.

He was right inside Clinker's stall now, his arm up around the horse's neck. Clinker shivered violently and seemed to shrink away from the familiar touch. Sophie crept cautiously in beside Grandpa and stared at the horse. Already his nose was swelling and the marks of the snake-bite were plain to see.

"Get up on those boards there, Sophie," said Grandpa. "I want you right away from his feet. I've got to cut into that bite to let the blood flow and he's not going to like it."

Sophie climbed up onto the boards that divided Clinker's stall from Bella's. Bella looked at her with puzzled eyes. Grandpa's sharp knife was out. He held Clinker's head firmly and cut at once into the ugly swelling—four strokes downwards, four strokes across. Clinker pulled his head back, tossing it desperately this way and that. He bared his teeth and showed the whites of his eyes. He reared up, neighing in fear, and snapped out at Grandpa's hand. Blood and poison flowed down together from the horse's nose. Sophie turned her eyes away and gripped on tighter to the boards where she sat.

Clinker was calmer now but shivering and sweating. His dark eyes were dull and cloudy. Slowly his legs began to give way beneath him and he crumpled heavily to the ground. He lay there on one side in his stall, his bleeding head on the straw. Sophie began to cry.

"Stop that, me darling," said Uncle Ted who had come in from finishing off the snake. His voice was kind but firm. "Grandpa's going to need a lot of help. You won't be much use to him if you're crying. I'll just move Bella further down the shed and we'll get these boards out of the way so Clinker's got more room in there. Come on, me darling. You can give me a hand."

Sophie was glad to have something to do. Once Bella was out of the way, Uncle Ted knocked out the boards from their slots and Sophie carried them to the other side of the stables.

"Get me some blankets, Sophie," Grandpa called to her from his place on the floor by Clinker's head. "You'll find them in the little shed next door. And Ted, I'll need that paraffin oil. Quick now, lad. We haven't got much time if we're going to save this poor old horse."

Uncle Ted and Sophie ran off together. She was back in two minutes with her arms stretched around a thick pile of grey horse-blankets. She held them out to Grandpa.

"More!" said Grandpa as he jumped up and took them from her. She ran for more. When she came back with her second load, Grandpa was spreading the blankets carefully over Clinker's shivering body and talking softly to him all the time. But Clinker didn't seem to hear him now. His eyes were closed and his mouth lay stiffly open. Sophie spread more blankets over his flanks and outstretched legs.

Uncle Ted ran in with the paraffin. Grandpa forced Clinker's jaws further apart, tilted back his head and poured the oil down his throat. Clinker coughed and choked. The paraffin dribbled out between his yellow teeth and soaked into the dirt floor.

"He can't swallow properly, that's the trouble," said Grandpa. "His throat's stiffened up already. I'll have another go."

Once more he pulled Clinker's jaw down and tipped the tin of oil. Not much was going down.

"I'll keep on with this stuff but we'll have to flush him out from the other end," said Grandpa. "Sophie, you run up to your Auntie Dot at the house. I want six gallons of warm soapy water. She'll have a few kettles on the boil and you can get a bucket of cold from the river. Call Queenie to help you, and give a couple of the men a shout. Ted, we need that stirrup pump. Where is it?"

"I know!" said Uncle Ted. "I'll get it!" He was out of the stable door before Sophie.

Up at the house Auntie Dot snatched her two steaming kettles off the stove.

"Queenie!" she shouted. "Go and ask Mrs Roberts for all her boiling water. Bring it to the stables. And Sophie, you'll find the buckets outside the back door!"

She was gone. Sophie filled the buckets and staggered from the river to the stables with her heavy load. Uncle Ted mixed the hot water with the cold in a deep tin tub and frothed it up with a block of soap in his hand.

"Keep lathering this water, Sophie!" he said. "I've got to work the pump."

Sophie only half watched what was happening out of the corner of her eye. She couldn't bear to look too closely but she couldn't bring herself to turn right away and miss it all. Gently Grandpa lifted Clinker's tail and pushed in the hose. Uncle Ted set to work, steadily pumping, his body rising and falling as he pulled and pushed on the handle. The soapy water surged into Clinker's body and out again, washing out everything with it.

Sophie handed the soap to Queenie and backed a bit further off. She could not bear to be so close. Clinker was lying completely still. He didn't seem aware of what was going on around him or of the water pumping into his bowels. Uncle Ted reached the bottom of the tin bath.

Grandpa groaned.

"There's nothing for it, Ted," he muttered. "We'll have to bleed him. You hold his head for me. Here's Jim Roberts. He can grab the bucket. Dot, you'd better get these two kids outside."

Sophie looked back for an instant as Auntie Dot shepherded her and Queenie through the door. She caught one terrifying glimpse of Grandpa driving some strange instrument hard into Clinker's neck. The dark blood gushed out into Jim Roberts' waiting bucket. Sophie ran, her stomach heaving.

Auntie Dot was exasperated.

"What a thing to happen on Christmas Day!" she said as they reached the house.

"I'm not eating any dinner, Ma!" said Queenie, as white as Sophie.

"Oh yes you are, my girl. I'm not having all that work for nothing. I've been slaving over that fire stove the whole morning and there's more to do yet. Go and have a sleep on your bed, the pair of you. You'll feel better in a couple of hours when I've got everything ready. Lottie and Effie can help me."

"But Auntie, Clinker might die!" sobbed Sophie, who could not stop her tears now.

"He might. But we're all going to eat a decent Christmas dinner just the same. Your Grandpa's the one who can save old Clinker if anyone can. He's saved a good few sick horses in his time. There's nothing more we can do."

Sophie and Queenie clung to each other in the bed and slept from exhaustion and shock. At one o'clock Auntie Dot called them to the table. To their surprise they did feel better. Grandpa was there and Uncle Ted, all washed and clean with their best clothes on and their hair sleeked down with water. Sophie didn't dare ask about Clinker for fear of hearing something dreadful.

"He's not dead yet," said Grandpa without waiting for her to ask. "But the trouble's not over. Not by a long chalk. It'll be touch and go for a couple of days, I reckon. Lucky you were quick off the mark with those blankets, Sophie. That was a real good help. And you kept your head too. You're a grand lass, all right. Just like your poor, dear mother."

Sophie wondered, as she'd often wondered at the mill, why everyone called her mother "poor". It was very puzzling and it made her feel sad but she pushed the question out of her head. She turned her mind quickly back to Clinker.

"Who's with him now, Grandpa? You haven't left him all alone down there, have you?"

"No, no. He's not alone. One of the lads is sitting with her for an hour or so just while I eat Dot's dinner here. Then I'll get on my working clothes again and back I'll go. You can come down with me if you like. Do the old horse good to hear your voice."

When the roast rabbits were eaten, then came Auntie Dot's great moment with her Christmas pudding. It was rather overshadowed for Sophie by the thought of Clinker lying sick in the stables. Still, it was a marvellous moment all the same. Nothing like that ever happened at the farm! They all sat around the long table waiting expectantly. Auntie herself had disappeared into the kitchen, her face red and perspiring from her morning over the hot oven and the boiling pots. Uncle Ted drew the thick curtains across the windows to shut out the fierce white sunlight. Then Auntie walked triumphantly into the darkness from the kitchen, the blazing pudding held high above her head in both hands. A sprig of gum leaves burned and crackled on top, filling the whole room with the sweet smoky smell of eucalyptus.

Sophie gasped as the blue flames licked up the sides of the pudding. They flared and flickered and went out. Everyone clapped and cheered. Uncle Ted pulled back the curtains as Auntie Dot sank, smiling and exhausted, into her chair, fanning herself happily with an old straw hat. Sophie felt tears prickling in her eyes but she couldn't tell why.

Queenie cut the pudding into slices.

"It's better than ever, me darling," cried Uncle Ted, taking his first mouthful. "And here's a threepenny bit!" He took the tiny silver coin from his mouth and rubbed it between his fingers.

Everyone found threepenny bits and Sophie found the ring. The steaming pudding, rich with raisins and spices and swimming in cream, was the most amazing food she had ever eaten but she was already so full she could hardly manage to swallow each wonderful mouthful.

"I'm going down to the stables again," announced Grandpa when all the pudding was eaten. "Coming, Sophie? And Queenie?"

Uncle Ted stood up slowly and reached for his hat.

"Well, me darling," he said to Auntie Dot without quite looking at her, "I'll be pushing off to the billiard shed now. The boys'll all be waiting for me."

An anxious frown creased Auntie Dot's face.

"Don't be too late, Ted," she said. "And make sure Jim Roberts gets home early too. His wife's having a hard time of it with that new baby of hers in all this heat. It never stops crying, poor thing."

Uncle Ted made no rash promises. With a sheepish smile and an awkward wave of his hand he was gone.

Sophie and Queenie took turns to sit with Grandpa in Clinker's stall all through the hot dry afternoon. There was a faint smell of bush-fires in the air, miles away but strangely sharp and smoky. When her turn came round, Sophie bathed Clinker's head with cool water and talked on and on to him, telling him the stories of all the books she'd ever read back at the farm. But Clinker did not move. His ears lay flat and still and his lidded eyes stayed shut. The weak breath struggled in and out of his lungs. Sophie stopped talking. He didn't seem to hear her any more.

8. The Midnight Bogie

By ten o'clock on Christmas night the noise from the billiard shed filled the darkness. Drunken singing and shouting, wild raucous laughter and sudden angry quarrels that flared up and faded away again. All the men from the mill were there apart from the boss himself and the others who'd gone off to Forrest or Colac or Birregurra for Christmas. Grandpa had looked in for half an hour early in the evening but now he sat on in the stables by Clinker, a solitary hurricane lantern burning beside him. In the grey houses along the hillside every light was out. The women and children were all in bed but not all asleep. The wives lay listening. How long would it go on? Here and there a child was crying, disturbed by the noise. Yellow light spilled out from the billiard shed windows.

Sophie couldn't sleep. The hot sheet lay heavily on her legs but she didn't like to throw it off in case she woke Queenie. She could hear Auntie Dot tossing about and muttering crossly to herself in the squeaky bed in the next room. The noise from the shed was frightening. Often it rose to a terrifying pitch, loud, violent and threatening. What are they doing down there, Sophie wondered. Are they all murdering each other? Then the noise sank down again to a grumbling distant murmur. One strong voice (was it Uncle Ted's?) would bellow out the words of some old song. The other voices shouted the chorus together, all out of time and tune.

Sophie heard a new sound. Footsteps were hurrying up the steps and along the verandah. Someone was knocking. The tapping on the door was soft but urgent.

"Mrs Blakeley!" whispered a woman's voice. "Are you awake?"

Sophie heard Auntie Dot heave herself out of bed and pad through the house to the door.

"Who is it? What's the matter?" she said.

"It's me. And the baby." The voice was crying now.

"Mrs Roberts! Come inside! Is the baby all right?"

"She's terribly sick. She needs the doctor," sobbed Mrs

Roberts. "And Jim's down there drinking himself stupid. What can I do?"

The baby began to wail. Queenie woke up suddenly and found Sophie at the end of the bed, listening and scared.

"Come on," said Queenie. "Let's see what's up."

She slid out of bed and Sophie followed her.

In the kitchen Mrs Roberts sat crying with her head in her hands and Auntie Dot held the baby, rocking it backwards and forwards in her arms, trying to quieten its howling. The baby was pale and thin with an ugly seeping rash around her neck.

"Queenie! Sophie!" said Auntie Dot when she saw them. "Thank goodness you're both awake. You'll have to go down to the shed to get Pa and Jim Roberts out of there. They might take more notice of you than they would of me. Tell them Jeannie's sick. She needs the doctor. They'll have to go to Forrest to get him. Tell them it's urgent. Off you run and don't come back without them. I'll make Mrs Roberts some tea."

Sophie and Queenie tore down the hill towards the lighted shed. High above them the enormous Christmas stars hung in a blue-black sky. Trig lay patiently outside the wide-open door with the other mill dogs, his eyes alert.

The girls stopped and looked in. Sophie shrank back. She could hardly believe what she saw in there. Men lay dead-drunk along the chairs or sprawled out on the dirty floor. The long green tree-fern fronds had been stripped from the walls and flung anyhow amongst the prostrate bodies. Uncle Ted was dancing along on the billiard table in his boots, a strand of white Christmas bush draped around his neck. His red hair was dishevelled and there was a peculiar smile on his face. A little group of men was singing together in one corner, their arms locked tight around each other's necks, swaying in a circle. The tap of one of the beer barrels had been left on and a pool of beer was spreading wider and wider across the earth floor.

"We can't go in there!" gasped Sophie, pulling Queenie back.

"We've got to! Jeannie's sick! Come on!" and Queenie marched into the room, stepping boldly over the bodies. Sophie crept cautiously after her. The mingled smells of beer and sweat were nauseating.

"Hullo there, me darlings!" called Uncle Ted, snatching up a fallen fern frond to wave at them. "Come on in and enjoy the fun!" His voice was thick and slurred. He seemed to Sophie a different person. She could hardly make out what he was saying.

"Pa!" said Queenie sternly, looking up at him. "Ma wants you to come home and Mr Roberts too. His baby's sick. You'll have to get the doctor!"

"Whasha'?" bawled one of the singing men and broke away from the group. "Who shays I have to go home?"

"Your baby's sick, Mr Roberts! Jeannie! She needs the doctor!" said Queenie, going up close to him and raising her voice to try to make him take it in.

"Baby? Wha' baby?" said Jim Roberts vacantly. He reeled back to the circle of singers, clamped his arms along their shoulders and began to move around again in the same old circle.

"Pa!" begged Queenie. "Please! *You* can come even if he can't. *You* could get the doctor. You're not too bad. You can still stand up."

"Not for long, me darling! Not for long! Me legs are giving way. I can feel 'em going!" And Uncle Ted sank slowly down onto the billiard table and lay there, completely silent and still.

"Pa! Wake up! Wake up!" Queenie shook him by the shoulder and rocked him from side to side, but he didn't move or speak.

"It's no good, Queenie!" said Sophie, dragging her back. "Let's get away from here! I hate it!"

Queenie was crying.

"Won't *any* of you come?" she shouted desperately at the singing circle of men. "The baby's sick! We need the doctor!"

"Go home, you dratted kids!" Jim Roberts shouted back and the dreary singing began again.

Sophie took Queenie's hand and led her out of the shed and back up the hill.

"They wouldn't come, Auntie!" she said at the kitchen door. "They're all too drunk! They don't care tuppence about the baby!"

Auntie Dot comforted Queenie who was sobbing with a mixture of rage and disappointment.

"We'll get the doctor ourselves then!" she said. "Be blowed to those men and their drink!"

"Auntie, why don't we *take* the baby to the doctor?" asked Sophie. "We could wrap her up well. We could drive one of the horses with a bogie. Any one of those timber trucks would do."

"I'm not coming!" sobbed Queenie.

"No, you don't have to come at all, dear," said Auntie Dot with her arm around her. "I need you to stay here to mind the little ones. Your Pa won't be out of that shed till the morning and I'll be back by then. Sophie, you can come with us. Mrs Roberts could do with a hand with her baby. You go back to bed, Queenie, and we'll get dressed. That's the first thing. We can't ride into Forrest in our nightgowns. The air might cool down a bit. We'll need something warm on."

Mrs Roberts hurried off home with the baby. As soon as Auntie Dot and Sophie were ready, they ran down the darkened track to the stables. The noise from the billiard shed was more subdued now but they gave it a wide berth. Mrs Roberts was waiting by the stable door already, her baby wrapped in a trailing white shawl. Inside, Grandpa sat half asleep in Clinker's stall, the lantern beside him. Auntie Dot roused him and explained it all.

"But *I'll* go for the doctor, Dot," he said at once. "Sophie here can mind the horse. She's a real good lass with the horses now and Clinker knows her well. He'll be all right with her."

"No, Dad," said Auntie Dot firmly. "You've done enough for one day. And we need Sophie to help with the baby. Just you harness up one of the horses for us. And put a few boards across the bogie for us to give us something better to sit on. We'll take Trig too. Where is he?"

"Outside the billiard shed," said Sophie. "He's waiting for Uncle Ted."

"He'll have a long wait," said Auntie Dot bitterly. "He'd be much better off with us. We could do with a dog on that lonely tram-track. Go and get him, Sophie."

Grandpa had decided on Bella. He lifted her great leather collar from its hook on the wall and led the horse outside. Auntie Dot held the lantern while he fitted the collar round Bella's broad shoulders and harnessed her up with straps and chains to the waiting bogie by the landing platform. He laid a few planks across from one side of the bogie to the other to make a floor. Mrs Roberts climbed on board with Jeannie and sat at the back with her legs stuck out in front of her. Trig jumped up to his usual place on the beam by Bella's tail. Sophie sat next to Mrs Roberts and Auntie Dot climbed onto the back beam with her hand ready to pull on the brake.

"Here!" said Grandpa. "Take this lantern, Sophie. And shine it ahead of you when you can. You can't be too careful on that track at night."

"What about the tunnel?" asked Sophie, suddenly remembering its sliminess and wishing she was safely back in bed.

"Don't you worry about the tunnel, lass. Bella knows what to do," said Grandpa reassuringly. "Just sit tight and she'll take you through."

"Gee up there, Bella!" called Auntie Dot, and with a sudden lurch the truck rolled forwards.

Sophie was glad of the lantern. She left her seat by Mrs Roberts and climbed up next to Trig with the lantern propped on the beam beside her. Its light fell forwards onto Bella's back legs as they moved steadily into the darkness ahead of them. It fell backwards too onto Mrs Roberts and Jeannie and onto Auntie Dot's dangling feet. Outside that little circle of light everything else seemed black. Gradually Sophie's eyes got used to the dark and she began to see the trunks of the trees, ghostly white beside the track. Above her head, beyond the leaves that almost met from left and right, she could just see the stars, still shining as bright as ever. But there was no moon.

Night or day made no difference to Bella. She plodded confidently along between the rails, rattling over the first bridge and into the long dark tunnel. The lantern lit up the wet mossy walls and the dripping roof. Sophie reached over with one hand to touch Trig. His coat was warm and comforting. Once they were out of the tunnel again, the night air was fresh and cool, heavy with the sweet smell of river ferns and gum leaves. To her surprise, Sophie felt suddenly happy. Her fears had gone. She forgot about the billiard shed and the drunken men. The night was too good a time to waste. Why did everyone always sleep it away, she wondered, as the lower branches brushed lightly against her, when they could be driving through the bush under the stars?

Bella quickened her pace and almost pranced across the bridges in her clanking shoes. She was enjoying herself too — off for a spree in the middle of the night with only an easy load behind her. But Auntie Dot and Mrs Roberts were lost in thought, sad and exhausted. The baby whimpered and Mrs Roberts pulled the shawl close.

"That's one trouble your poor mother never has, Sophie," said Auntie Dot after a long silence.

"What is?"

"The drink. But then she's got troubles enough of her own."

"Has she?" said Sophie and wondered what troubles Auntie could mean.

"Your Uncle Ted's a good man for most of the year. It's only at Christmas that he goes too far. The others egg him on. That's really all it is." Her voice had lost its anger now. She seemed to be making excuses for him. "It's a hard life at the mill, you see, but I wouldn't change it for all the world and neither would he, I reckon."

With a jerk that almost knocked the lantern from Sophie's grasp, Bella stopped abruptly in her tracks and whinnied loudly, her head high in the air. Auntie Dot grabbed at the brake.

"Gee up there, Bella!" she called sharply, but Bella stood still.

Auntie Dot jumped down and took the lantern from Sophie. She walked along beside Bella, one hand on the horse's flank. She shone the light onto the tramway ahead. Sophie ran behind her, keeping close. There in front of them lay an enormous gum tree, its leafy branches spread out wide and its thick trunk crushing the rails.

"What can we do?" cried Sophie. "Bella can't get over that!"

Mrs Roberts climbed off the bogie and came to look, the whimpering baby held high on her shoulder.

"We'll have to walk," said Auntie Dot.

"How far is it?" asked Sophie.

"Not so far. We've come about four miles already. There must be two miles still to go."

"But what about Bella?"

"We'll just have to leave her here. She'll come to no harm for an hour or two. On the way back we'll have to harness her up

to the other end of the truck."

"But Auntie, do you know how to do it?"

"Of course I do, Sophie," laughed Auntie Dot. "I'm not a fool, you know. I grew up on a farm, just like your mother. We learnt a thing or two about horses in those days. Come on now. We mustn't waste time."

Sophie found herself wondering again about Mother. Did she really ever know how to handle horses? If so, then why did Dad keep her right away from them now? It was a mystery.

Auntie Dot loosened Bella's harness and rubbed the horse's nose.

"Good girl," she said. "You stopped in the nick of time. We won't be long. Just wait for us. Come on, Trig. We need you."

Trig bounded up to her.

Auntie Dot took the lantern again and held it high over her head, trying to make out how far the big tree reached.

"We'll have to skirt right around it," she said at last. "We can't get over those branches. The top must be somewhere right down the side of the gully. It's fairly steep but we can manage. Just follow me."

Auntie Dot dived off to the right of the tram-track down a sharp slope towards the creek, the swaying lantern throwing strange lights and shadows over the leaves of the fallen tree. Trig dashed ahead. Sophie and Mrs Roberts slipped and scrambled down together. It was a long way down to the very top of the tree but they turned around it at last and began the climb up on the far side. Once they had reached the tramway again they set off in a little procession — Auntie Dot in front with the lantern and Trig, then Sophie in the middle and Mrs Roberts with the baby last of all. The white shawl trailed almost to the ground.

Sophie's excitement had vanished. She had felt so safe on the bogie and the night had seemed so lovely but now that she was walking wearily along behind Auntie Dot, her feet thumping on the sleepers one by one, the bush around seemed far less friendly. She started and caught her breath each time a bird squawked in the trees. She heard or thought she heard the rustle of some big animal pushing through the bracken. Even the little creek, splashing over its hidden stones, sounded menacing now. And when they came to the next narrow bridge, Sophie could not bear even to think of the terrifying deep drop on either side but crept along slowly in the dead centre of the track, not looking to left or to right, simply putting one foot carefully in front of the other.

"Hurry up, Sophie! You're dragging," Auntie Dot called back over her shoulder. "It's not far now."

Mrs Roberts stumbled.

"Would you like me to take the baby?" asked Sophie, though she'd never held a baby in her life before.

Without a word, Mrs Roberts put Jeannie in Sophie's arms.

At first the tiny bundle seemed as light as air but with every five mintues that passed the baby grew heavier. Sophie's arms ached but she tried to think about her feet, not her arms. She must not fall.

"A light!" called Auntie Dot. "We're nearly there! That's the station just ahead of us."

When they reached the platform and climbed up to it from the tram-track, Sophie handed Jeannie back to Mrs Roberts.

"That baby's very quiet," said Auntie Dot suspiciously. She came and peered in at the little white face.

"She's all right," said Mrs Roberts. "I can feel her breathing. Where's the doctor's house?"

"This way," said Auntie Dot and strode confidently down the dusty main street, rounded iron verandah roofs on each side. All the lights were out in the general store, the bank and the dark line of houses. Auntie Dot kept to the middle of the road.

"There's the place," she said. "The white gate at the corner."

Sophie and Mrs Roberts followed her up the short flagged path to the verandah steps. The garden was full of lavender. Sophie couldn't see it but she smelt it, strong and fresh in the cool night air. Auntie Dot knocked at the door—once, twice.

"Dr Steen!" she called. "We've got a sick baby here."

Someone inside the house lit a candle that flickered at the window. Sophie could hear soft footsteps coming to the door. It opened and there stood the doctor's wife in a long white nightgown, her grey hair hanging down over her shoulders.

"Who is it?" she asked, gazing out at the three strange figures on the verandah and holding her candle higher to get a better look at them.

"It's just me, Mrs Steen. Mrs Blakeley from Stringybark Mill. And here's Mrs Roberts with a sick baby. We need the doctor."

"Oh, Mrs Blakeley! I can see you now. I just didn't recognize you in the dark. Do come in, all of you. He's getting out of bed now." She led the way into the house and lit the kitchen lamp.

"And this must be Queenie!" she said, looking at Sophie with surprised eyes. "She *has* changed since the last time I saw her!"

Auntie Dot laughed.

"No, it's not Queenie at all! That's my niece, Sophie. She's with us for Christmas."

Mrs Steen smiled at Sophie.

"I'll make some tea. Mrs Roberts, you sit here. You look worn out. How on earth did you get here?"

"Half way on a timber-truck with Bella pulling us," said Auntie Dot, "and the rest of the way on foot. There was a tree down across the line."

"All in the dark! Along that tram-track! Nothing in the world would drag me out there at night!"

"We're used to the bush," said Auntie Dot, sinking gratefully into a chair. "But I must admit I'm glad to be here."

Dr Steen came into the room. He was half dressed with his shirt buttons still undone and no shoes on his feet. He was a tall thin man with grey hair and beard. His spectacles were pushed up to his forehead. He didn't say much but took the baby from Mrs Roberts and laid it down gently on the kitchen table. He moved each limb in turn, looked closely into her eyes, listened to her breathing, felt her pulse and examined the raw rash around her neck. It was spreading now down over her chest and arms.

"Don't worry, Mrs Roberts," he said at last. "You've come in good time. It's a heat rash and heat exhaustion. I think you and the baby had better stay with us for a few days. You could do with a rest yourself and the baby's going to need constant care."

"But I can't possibly stay! I don't want to be such a bother to you. And then there's my husband to look after at the mill." Mrs Roberts' pale face was drawn tight with worry.

"Don't you worry about him!" said Auntie Dot. "When he's

sobered up, I'll feed him for you. No doubt he'll be in here to see you with a face as long as a fiddle!"

"And it's no trouble to us at all," said Mrs Steen, pouring out five cups of strong tea. "The bed's always made up and ready. It's a pleasure to have you — and the little baby too. Now here's the tea and some Christmas cake."

Jeannie began to wail again, a thin plaintive cry. Mrs Roberts wrapped her firmly in the shawl and rocked her till the noise stopped. The tea was good and hot. The cake was rich and dark and spicy. Sophie wanted to go on sitting there at the kitchen table all night, sipping and munching in comfort, but Auntie Dot had finished her cup already and was standing up.

"We must be getting back, Mrs Steen. Poor old Bella's waiting for us down the track. We can't leave her too long. Come on, Sophie."

Trig was lying patiently on the front verandah. Auntie Dot lit the lantern again and in a few minutes she and Sophie were hurrying back along the shadowy street towards the station. The walk down the tramway seemed easier this time. Sophie's legs ached but her fears had gone now that the baby was safe and they were on their way home. When they reached the tree and called to Bella, Auntie Dot almost ran down the steep side of the gully to the topmost branches near the water's edge and up the other side. Sophie panted behind her, slipping on the bracken as she ran. There was Bella, standing as still as a stone in the dark. Auntie Dot led her round to the far end of the bogie and harnessed her up again. The heavy chains clanked as she swung them into place. She climbed on board with Sophie and Trig beside her. She released the brake and shouted out to Bella. The big horse moved off and the truck began to roll. Bella's hoofs struck hard on the sleepers with a comforting sound that echoed through the night.

Sophie leant against Auntie Dot and fell asleep. She didn't see the swaying bridges at all or the dripping tunnel or the fading stars. She woke with a start as the bogie burst out of the bush and into the little mill township just as day was breaking. The houses looked pale and almost white in the early morning light. Down at the billiard shed a line of drooping men was coming slowly out through the door. They rubbed their eyes and moved their heads stiffly, looking about them as if they wondered where they were and how on earth they'd got there. They shuffled uneasily up the hill to their houses. Uncle Ted was the last to emerge. He stood amazed by the billiard shed, watching Auntie Dot and Sophie climb off the truck. He kept standing and gazing as they led Bella back to the stables. Grandpa still sat on his stool in Clinker's stall, his head slumped on his chest, half asleep. He jerked awake at the sound of Bella's hoofs on the straw. Sophie ran to look at Clinker. He was breathing peacefully, his flanks rising and falling easily. Sophie felt his coat. The fever had gone. Grandpa smiled at her.

Uncle Ted shambled behind them into the stables.

"Where've you been, me darling?" he asked as Auntie Dot gave Bella her water and oats and rubbed down her back and legs.

"We went for the doctor, Ted. Mrs Roberts' baby was sick. Remember?" Auntie Dot laughed bitterly. Her voice was hard.

"I don't remember a thing!" he said in bewilderment, looking from Sophie to Auntie Dot and back again. He winced in pain when he moved his head.

"It's Christmas, Ted. You were having a few drinks with the boys in the billiard shed."

"Christmas!" exclaimed Uncle Ted. "Now I remember!" His face flushed. He put one big arm awkwardly around Auntie Dot's shoulder.

"I'm sorry, Dot, me darling! It'll never happen again."

Auntie Dot laughed, more happily now but wearily too.

"That's just what you said last year, Ted. Come on. Let's have breakfast. Then I want some sleep and so does Sophie."

The settlement at Stringybark Mill dozed in the heat. At dinner time, just as Sophie and Queenie were bringing fresh water from the river for Clinker to drink, Mr Greenbank and his wife walked in along the tramway. They'd had to leave their horse and timber truck back beyond the fallen tree.

He took one look inside the billiard shed door at all the mess and shook his head.

"I said we should never have gone off and left them to it, Min," he said to his wife. "If only we'd stayed here for

Christmas Day we could've stopped it."

"Nothing could've stopped it, Bill! Nothing and no one! I'm thankful we were out of the way. And who's going to clear it up? Not the women, anyway! They've had quite enough to put up with by the look of it."

"I'll get the men onto it straight away. They made the place a shambles—they can clean it up. And I'll have to send a gang of loggers down the tram-track to move that tree. Where *are* all the men, Queenie?" he called across to her where she stood with Sophie at the stable door.

"Sleeping it off, Mr Greenbank. Pa's lying on our verandah. Ma said she wasn't having those boots on the bed and he couldn't bend down to take them off."

"I'll go round the houses myself and wake them up!" said Mr Greenbank grimly. "They've had a fair go. There'll be no Sports Day for them in a couple of weeks if this filthy shed isn't spick and span by tea time!"

Mr Greenbank did the rounds of the little grey houses, pounding mercilessly on every front door until all the men, bleary-eyed and sullen, came out one by one, blinking painfully in the fierce white sunlight. The logging crew harnessed up three of the horses to a couple of timber trucks and bowled off along the Forrest track with their saws and axes to cut up the tree and mend the broken rails. They weren't singing on the job today. They sat silent, back to back along their bogies, their black hats pulled well down on their heads, their legs dangling over the side.

The mill crew began slowly to clear up the billiard shed with Mr Greenbank lending a hand. The bedraggled fern fronds and the wilting strands of Christmas bush were heaped together near the river's edge to be burned off later when the weather was cooler. The empty beer barrels were loaded onto a truck ready for the run back to Forrest the next day. The windows were opened up, the floor swept clean and the billiard table set to rights again in the middle of the shed. The smell of beer still lingered on.

"Well, that's Christmas over," said Queenie sadly as she and Sophie sat in the shade of the stable wall and watched the men at work.

"But Clinker didn't die," said Sophie. "That's the best

Christmas present of all. Grandpa says he'll be all right in a couple of weeks if we look after him well."

"And Pa killed that snake," said Queenie with satisfaction.

9. *Sports Day*

New Year's Day came quietly at the mill. Some families had gone away to stay with relations for the two week break. The few men who were left did odd jobs on the bridges and the tram-tracks for extra pay. Mrs Price had shut up her kitchen school for the last time and the mill children ran free all over the settlement and splashed about in the river to cool off. Rabbiting and fishing took them well out into the bush and up to the deep pools in Coldwater Creek. Still the long dry heat wave rose higher and higher, day after day.

Sophie couldn't quite believe that a new year had really come. She didn't feel any different. Everything at the mill looked exactly the same. 1909! It sounded very odd and it even looked odd when she wrote it for the first time at the head of her weekly letter to Mother. What would this new year bring, she wondered? The baby? Sophie pushed the uncomfortable thought right out of her mind.

A week later, everyone was back home at the mill and getting ready for Sports Day in Forrest. Little Jeannie Roberts was better and even she was going to Sports Day. Only old Clinker had to be left behind. He was well over the worst now but he still wasn't strong enough for the walk into Forrest or for racing around the paddock with the others. He'd just have to be tethered in the shade near the mill within easy reach of the river and a patch of grass.

Sophie and Queenie were both up at six to help Grandpa and Ray Sanders get the horses ready. Most of the men were there early to lend a hand. The horses were fed and watered, brushed and combed. By eight every tail and mane had been plaited with red ribbon twined in and out among the wiry hair; every coat was groomed till it shone in the sunshine; the thick white feather around every fetlock was clean and smooth; every leather collar was polished with wax and decorated with red rosettes. The harness gleamed and even the heavy chains looked festive as they linked every team of three or four horses to one of the timber trucks. Planks were laid across the bogies to give the people somewhere to sit for the journey along the track to Forrest.

All the mill families climbed on board, laden with picnic baskets, saws and axes for the competitions, straw sun-hats, rugs to spread at the sports ground and nosebags stuffed with oats for the horses. Mr Greenbank gave the signal from the front wagon, the children cheered and Diamond stepped out proudly at the head of the splendid procession. The four crowded bogies rolled. Sophie sat with Queenie at the back of the last truck. She wanted to have one final glimpse of Clinker by the water as the bush swallowed them up and the mill township disappeared from sight.

Horse followed horse, truck followed truck. Singing and laughing, legs dangling and swinging, the mill people were pulled along the tramway to Forrest. The day was hot and sticky with a hint of thunder in the air. The smoky smell of distant bush fires still lingered. But this was Sports Day and no worry about rain or fire could dispel the mounting excitement on board the trucks.

"I haven't been into Forrest since last Sports Day," said Queenie.

"Not even once! In a whole year!" Sophie was surprised.

"Well, how often do you go into Birregurra?"

"Not often," admitted Sophie. "Only two or three times a year. But Mother goes every week. To do the shopping."

"We don't need to go shopping in Forrest. We've got all we want in the store at the mill. But Sports Day's different. Everyone's there from all over the Otways. They even come down all the way from Colac on a special train. Plenty come from Birregurra. Your Dad could be there, even."

Sophie shook her head and laughed at the very thought.

The special train from Colac was already in the station at Forrest and the crowds were surging along the little platform. The Stringybark men unhooked their horses and led them in a slow column along the main street to the sports ground by the river. Women and children trailed behind the horses with the picnic things. Every sawmill in the district had closed for the day and every sawmiller had brought his axe and his saw to Forrest. The crew from Sanderson's mill was there and the men from Robins' mill at Barramunga with all their families. They were there from Hayden's mills and from McGregor's and from Mackie Creek.

They came from Henry's and from Armistead's, from Rickett's Clearing and from Turton Track.

Sophie was amazed that they all seemed to know each other even though most of them only gathered together once a year at Forrest. They hailed each other from buggies and horseback and from the groups that moved along the road on foot with the heavy horses.

"Our team looks the best," said Queenie, casting a critical eye over the lines of horses from the other mills.

The sports ground was simply a wide paddock cleared of trees and stumps. The tussocky dry grass, mown down to a wiry stubble, was rough under foot. All along the river side of the paddock stood a row of open booths and tents made from greyish tarpaulins strung across rough wooden frames. At one end were a couple of large marquees already set out with trestle tables.

The men from Stringybark led their horses to the far end of the paddock where a thick row of trees provided shade from the sun. The women found a place to spread the rugs and sit. The children careered wildly up and down, shouting out excitedly to everyone they knew, dashing in and out of the empty booths.

"What are they for?" asked Sophie, looking along the line of tents.

"Those smaller ones are for changing in before the races and competitions. Up the top are the two big ones. There'll be tea in one of them and beer in the other. Come on, I'll show you," and she led Sophie into the beer tent where there was no sign yet of any beer.

"Clear out of here, you kids!" called a large sweating man cheerfully as he ran in rolling a beer barrel beside him. Eight other men with identical barrels rolled in after him. Sophie and Queenie made for the door.

"There's the bookie down there," said Queenie. "That's his tent in the middle of the row. He takes bets on all the events. Pa reckons the bookie's the only one who ever makes any money out of Sports Day."

"Who are all those men up the top near the horses? Look, Queenie, under the trees. They've all got packs and bags."

"They're just the hawkers. They come from all over the district today. See how they've each got a patch pegged out on the grass? That's how the miners used to peg out their gold claims, Pa says. In the old days."

Uncle Ted and Grandpa were helping to set out white hurdles in the centre of the paddock to mark out the lanes and squares for the competitions. The tent for the judges' box was erected on the far side, opposite all the changing booths. Blocks of wood were dragged in for the chopping and sawing contests, piles of hessian bags for the sack races, tubs of old potatoes and bundles of red flags. Sophie felt a new kind of excitement rising from somewhere inside her.

"When does it all start?" she said, hopping from one foot to the other.

"Any minute now. Let's find Ma. She'll have a good place for the rug and the baskets."

Sophie settled down on the rug with Auntie Dot and the children.

"First event of the day, ladies and gentlemen," boomed a voice through a kind of trumpet. "We're starting with the kiddies as usual. Boys under eight. Flat race. All boys to the top of the paddock please. The starters are waiting for you."

A swarm of little boys ran barefoot to the starting line, some in short trousers, others in long trousers rolled up to the knee. Even Bertie toddled along behind them, pushed by Lottie and Effie.

The whistle blew as the red flag fell. They were off. Sports Day had begun.

Race followed race down the paddock. Girls staggered along clutching bags up under their armpits; ladies hobbled past in their long skirts with eggs balanced on spoons; men leaped hurdles and passed flags and scooped up potatoes. Sophie had never seen anything like it. At first she wouldn't get up with Queenie to join in, but bit by bit she felt less timid.

"Go on, Sophie, have a try!" urged Lottie when the over-twelves hoop race was announced through the trumpet. Sophie got up slowly. She knew she was quite good at hoops — at least at home on the flat dusty road to the farm. Bumpy grass was another matter but she followed Queenie to the starting line and the great pile of hoops.

Two minutes later Sophie was flying down the paddock with

her iron hoop bouncing almost out of control at her side and the crowd roaring its encouragement to the runners. Suddenly Sophie wanted to win. She pushed herself harder, spun her hoop deftly with a quick flick of her hand and strained forward to the finishing rope. Queenie's hoop was down. Sophie ran on. The crowd shouted. She'd done it! She'd won the hoop race by yards and yards. The other girls panted in behind her, poor Queenie last of all.

"Well done, me darling!" Uncle Ted's loud voice carried right down to her from one end of the paddock to the other. Sophie's face was burning red with pleasure and pride. And with embarrassment too. She wasn't used to being at the centre of everyone's attention.

"Wood-chopping events! All competitors to the ring, please!" bellowed the man with the trumpet. Sophie's brief moment of glory was over already. She knew what Dad would say if she told him she'd won the hoop race.

"Every dog has its day," he'd mutter with a shrug and he'd turn to look out of the window again, towards the same old knot of cows in the home paddock.

As the wood-choppers poured onto the paddock now, Sophie couldn't help remembering with a painful start how Mother always lifted up Dad's heavy axe every Monday morning at the farm. Was she still chopping the wood on washing days, Sophie wondered? And who would do it when the baby was born?

"Look," cried Queenie in excitement. "They're starting!"

Sophie pushed all thoughts of the farm from her mind.

With coats off and shirt sleeves rolled up, the sawmillers from Stringybark and from Sanderson's and Robins' and Hayden's, from McGregor's and from Henry's, from Mackie Creek and Armistead's, from Rickett's Clearing and from Turton Track wielded their axes to chop through the solid standing blocks and heaved back and forth on their cross-cut saws to slice through the thick horizontal logs. Betting was fast and furious and the beer tent did a roaring trade. Sophie and Queenie sat and sipped their raspberry vinegar as they watched, and bit into their wedges of Auntie Dot's sponge cake with cream oozing out at the sides. Sophie turned for a minute to gaze at the happy crowd. Her eye was caught by a couple of latecomers, labouring up the edge of the paddock in hot town clothes.

"Queenie!" she exclaimed with her mouth still full of cake. "There's that Mr Hooker again! Look! And Mr Drake too with his blue bag! What are they doing here?"

Queenie's eyes followed Sophie's pointing finger.

"Everyone's here," she said and went on eating.

Mr Hooker, in his large flapping overcoat, was clearly looking for something or someone. With Norm Drake trotting close at his heels, he poked his head inside every tent and booth along the side of the sports ground. At the beer tent they disappeared altogether but came out a few minutes later looking dishevelled from pushing through the crowd. At the tea tent they simply stood at the open door and gazed up and down the long trestle tables. Sophie saw Norm Drake step eagerly inside but Mr Hooker pulled him back with one long arm and a firm shake of his head. The two men stood still and puzzled. Their eyes searched the teeming crowd. Then Mr Hooker gave a sudden jerk of recognition and set off loping over the grass towards the big horses. There must have been more than a hundred horses up there under the trees, lapping water from canvas buckets or steadily munching their oats. Mr Greenbank was standing by the Stringybark horses, his hand on Diamond's neck and talking with Ray Sanders. The time was getting near for the horse races and then the Grand Parade.

Mr Greenbank caught sight of the two men. He moved away from Diamond and strode forward to meet them. After much vigorous hand-shaking, the three of them walked slowly together to a quiet corner of the paddock, Mr Hooker and Mr Greenbank in front and Norm Drake just behind them with his bag, straining forward to catch every word of the conversation.

"I wonder what they're selling this time?" said Sophie.

"I don't think they're selling anything," said Queenie. "They're not real hawkers or they would've been here earlier. They're not even opening up their bag. I don't know what they are. Let's keep our eyes on them."

Mr Hooker and Mr Greenbank were talking earnestly together. They were almost arguing by the look of it. Norm Drake seemed worried. He hovered close beside them, shifting from one foot to the other and passing his bag from left hand to right and back again.

Suddenly Mr Greenbank was all smiles. He shook Mr Hooker by the hand again and clapped Norm Duke on the back.

"Well whatever it is, it's over and done with," said Queenie. "I bet they'll have a drink now. You watch. They'll make for the beer tent.

But Queenie was wrong. Mr Greenbank hurried back to his horses, looking decidedly pleased with himself, and the other two men made for the gate and past the row of buggies. Mr Hooker had taken the bag now and he steered Norm Drake along by his elbow, talking to him all the time. Norm Drake nodded his head.

"They're probably heading for the afternoon train," said Queenie. "Funny they didn't even stay for a drink."

The two men had reached the dusty road and were hurrying, almost running, towards the station.

"Horse races," roared the man with the trumpet.

Sophie and Queenie forgot all about Mr Hooker and his mate.

The sprightly riding horses came first, leaping the wooden hurdles the whole length of the paddock with lean young farmers in the saddle. Then it was the moment for the heavy horses, with daring sawmillers on their backs, to lumber around the sports ground. Even Grandpa was mounted on one of the Stringybark horses. He sat at the starting line with his back as straight and firm as a gum sapling and his old leathery hands grasping Bella's mane. The whistle blew and the big horses were off! The ground shook under those thundering hooves.

"Come on, Grandpa!" shouted Sophie, jumping up and down in excitement.

He didn't win but he ran a good race. Lots of the men fell off on the turn but not Grandpa.

"Ma says it could be his last Sports Day," said Queenie sadly.

"Why? He's better than most of the others," protested Sophie, sitting down on the grass again.

"I know. But he's getting on, Ma says. His bones are too brittle. He can't go on riding horses forever."

"Sophie Ramsdale!" exclaimed a familiar voice right behind them.

Sophie swung round, a ring of pink raspberry vinegar still

staining her mouth. A plump smiling face was beaming down at her.

"It's Mrs Dunphy!" she exclaimed in amazement. "I didn't know you came to Forrest for Sports Day!"

"Of course we do, love. Come every year. Never missed it yet."

Mrs Dunphy sank down beside the girls and taking off her broad-brimmed straw hat she fanned herself vigorously.

"Everyone's here from Birregurra and all the farms up our way— except your Dad, Sophie. *He* never comes. Sophie, I must tell you. I saw your mother just yesterday. It can't be long now. Poor woman, she's as big as a barn—and in all this heat too. What a time to have a baby!"

"There's a cool change coming, Pa says," put in Queenie, her eyes opening wide at the thought of anyone as big as a barn. "The clouds are building up."

"Let's hope it comes in time for Sophie's mother, then," said Mrs Dunphy, taking off her tight boots and lying right back on the prickly grass.

"Get me a cup of tea from the tent, love," she said to Sophie. "I'm fair stonkered!"

Sophie herself was far from stonkered. The day couldn't last long enough for her. When the heavy horses had finished their race and the trick riders came on standing upright in their saddles as their light horses leapt the hurdles, she thought she must be imagining things.

"Clinker'll never believe that if I tell him tonight," she said.

"Yes he will," laughed Queenie. "He's seen it every year. And he's seen the musical chairs on horseback—that comes next."

After the amazing musical chairs came the last event of all—the Grand Parade of the heavy horses from the mills. Mrs Dunphy sat up again. This was something that she couldn't miss.

The horses from Sanderson's mill were the first onto the paddock, all brushed and plaited, their harness twinkling in the sun that sank lower and lower in the sky. Their horseman led the first horse and the rest trotted along meekly behind and showed off all their paces. Then came the team from Hayden's Mill and next the nineteen horses from Stringybark. They were the biggest team. To Sophie's eyes they were by far the best. Their heads were held higher, their hoofs moved more nimbly, their coats shone in blacks and whites and browns and greys.

"Hurray!" she shouted, waving to Ray and Grandpa as they led the mighty work-horses right round the edge of the paddock.

"You seem quite at home with them big horses anyway, love," said Mrs Dunphy. "Your mother will be surprised."

"But you haven't seen Clinker, Mrs Dunphy," said Sophie seriously, as the teams from the other mills thundered past one by one. "He's the best horse of all!"

"Well I never!" exclaimed Mrs Dunphy, looking at Sophie's flushed and happy face in surprise.

The Sports Day had to end at last. It was almost sunset when the row of tents was pulled down and the hurdles stacked away. The buggies set off for the farms and townships. Heavy horses pulled drayloads of families back along the roads to the sawmills and from Forrest station the horse-drawn bogies rolled down the tramways into the bush to the isolated mills in the gullies. The special train chugged back to Colac.

This time Sophie had climbed onto the front truck behind Diamond, Bella and Sandy. Most of the mothers and children were on the two leading bogies. The men, all rather the worse for their visits to the beer tent, filled up the two at the back. Dark storm clouds had been building up in the sky all through the late afternoon and now they loomed blacker still as the last light faded. A sharp flash of lightning leapt high above the trees and a long low rumble of thunder announced that the storm was on its way.

From the very last bogie of all, Uncle Ted began to sing. His strong voice carried along the whole length of the procession. The men joined in the chorus and even the women and children were singing as soon as they had picked up the words.

I used to be a sailor, I sailed the ocean wide,
The captain was a tyrant and he worked me till I cried,
He chased me up the top mast and he flogged me with the cat,
So I jumped the ship in Melbourne and I made for Ballarat.

So now I am a wanderer, a swaggie on the track,
I sleep beneath the stars and hump me bluey on me back.

I used to be a miner, I used to delve for gold,
A'pickin' and a'shovellin' in sunshine and in cold,
I found a whackin' nugget and I showed it to me chum,
He pinched the damn thing off of me and sold it cheap for rum.

So now I am a wanderer, a swaggie on the track,
I sleep beneath the stars and hump me bluey on me back.

I used to be a farmer, a cocky on the land,
I had a team of horses and I kept 'em well in hand,
The droughts dried up me paddocks and the mice ate up me grain,
Me cattle died in hundreds and me tanks ran out of rain.

So now I am a wanderer, a swaggie on the track,
I sleep beneath the stars and hump me bluey on me back.

I used to be a woodman, way down at Stringybark,
I swung me axe above me head from morning up till dark,
The boss he was a decent bloke, he paid us on the nail,
But I drank too much one Christmas and he sent me off to jail.

So now I am a wanderer, a swaggie on the track,
I sleep beneath the stars and hump me bluey on me back.

Uncle Ted's song ended with a roar of laughter from the men's truck. Sophie could hear Mr Greenbank's voice above all the others.

"Well done, Ted," he shouted. "A good song and a good day! And here's the storm! Get a move on up there in front!"

The horses quickened their pace a little, sensing rain in the air as the thunder rolled closer. Sheets of lightning lit up the bush for an instant at a time so that Sophie could clearly see the white tree trunks beside the track. The first big drops began to fall, splashing down slowly onto the dry leaves and the parched earth.

Then with a violent crack that seemed to split the black sky open, the full force of the storm was on them, pouring down thick pelting rain onto bare heads and felt hats and thin cotton dresses. Sophie was soaked to the skin in minutes. Her dark hair was streaming. She clung tight to Auntie Dot, terrified by the wind lashing the trees and the violent explosions of thunder above them. Little Bertie was crying.

"Ma!" shouted Queenie above the tumult of the storm and quite untroubled by it. "What was it that Pa was telling you back there at the Forrest station? Something about Mr Greenbank."

"He says the boss has got a wonderful surprise for us all!" Auntie Dot shouted back, wiping the running water from her eyes. "It's coming to the mill next week!"

"What is it?" bellowed Queenie.

"I don't know. Your Pa doesn't know either. He thinks it might be a brand new saw for the mill but I think it's the schoolie—the teacher for our Stringybark school."

"He wouldn't come so early, Ma. School doesn't start till February."

"He'd want to settle in. He's a married man. There's that nice place all ready for him next to the school-house."

"It might be a new horse, Ma. Clinker's getting a bit old and he's been sick. We could do with another one."

"Or a few cows," suggested Sophie, lifting her voice above the rain, "for the milk."

"We'll just have to wait and see!" called Auntie Dot. "Mr Greenbank's not telling. Look, Queenie, here's the tunnel. We'll be dry in there for a couple of minutes, anyway."

The tunnel was quiet and cold. Sophie shivered. Then the horses trotted heavily out into the open again, their big feet splashing in the water between the rails, and the storm whipped around them again. When the trucks all reached the mill at last, the houses were invisible behind the darkness and the rain. Sophie could just make out Clinker's shadowy form where he stood patiently under his tree by the swirling river.

Sophie and Queenie were soon dry and comfortable and tucked up in their bed. Lottie and Effie fell asleep at once. Bertie was talking to himself in Grandpa's bed. A pile of wet bedraggled clothes lay on the front verandah. Down at the stables Uncle Ted and Grandpa were helping Ray Sanders to rub the horses dry and to calm their jumpy nerves. Auntie Dot sat alone in the kitchen drinking her last cup of tea for the day.

10. Mr Greenbank's Surprise

The rain poured down relentlessly all night long. Sophie lay in bed in the early morning and listened to it beating on the iron roof overhead. The tank by the back door was filling up again. The water splashed and gurgled as it surged along the guttering and into the down-pipe.

For three whole days and nights the rain kept up. The drought had really broken. All the little paths between the houses at the mill were streaming with water. The river was overflowing its banks and the flat stepping-stones were submerged. The men came back from the logging covered in mud from head to foot.

Clinker still had to stay in the stables each day when the other horses splashed off into the bush. He needed another week's rest, Grandpa said, and then he'd be fit for work again. Sophie had been running down to see him every morning since the day of the snake-bite. Even the rain didn't stop her. With an old newspaper over her head she slithered down the path straight after breakfast and rushed to the stables. They were empty except for Clinker in his stall. She called to him from the doorway as she eased the door open. He turned his head slowly to look at her and she climbed up onto the partition between his stall and the next. Grandpa was generally there before her, giving the horse a brisk rub down and filling his manger with oats. The rain trickled in under the walls and ran into sticky puddles on the hard earth floor.

"Why don't you get up on his back, Sophie?" said Grandpa on the first wet morning. "He can't take you out for a proper ride in all this rain but he likes to feel you're close. It helps him get better. Here, I'll give you a hand across." And Grandpa guided Sophie's legs as she stepped across the gap from her fence to slide onto Clinker's warm back. The horse went on placidly munching his oats. His big feet never moved an inch.

Sophie sat there for hours while the rain came down. As soon as Grandpa had left the stables she started talking to Clinker, her head down near his pricked ear. This seat was far better than her branch on the oak tree at home. An oak tree couldn't listen but she was sure that Clinker listened though he hardly ever opened his mouth to whinny or snuffle in reply. Sophie grew bolder. The ground didn't seem as far away as it used to do and she could slip off safely by herself to stand by the horse's head to stroke the white flash between his eyes.

When the rain stopped at last and the hot yellow sun rose in a clear blue sky again, the bush smelt steamy and damp. The brilliant birds that had been so hidden and silent through the long dry heat and the downpour now sprang into noise and life around the mill township. Before the new heat wave had time to build up again, everyone at the mill had burst of new energy. Auntie Dot gave the house a good clean out and Uncle Ted mended broken saws at his forge. The stables were opened up to the fresh air again and the mud-caked legs of the horses were washed down in the flooding river. Grandpa led Clinker gently up and down all the paths in the settlement with Sophie sitting confidently astride his back, just one of her hands lying lightly on his mane. The old spring was coming back into his step. Grandpa's stick tapped rhythmically in front of them as they walked. Sophie waved and called out to every family they passed. Mothers were hoeing the wet gardens or shaking out mats across the verandah rail; children and dogs were playing together in the muddy back yards or setting off to go rabbiting with their scuttling ferrets in a basket. Sophie knew all the people now and they knew her. As Clinker plodded and squelched along the little tracks up and down the hillside, Sophie suddenly saw herself, just for a fleeting minute or two, as if she was outside herself and looking down at this figure of a girl on a great draught horse. How strange, she thought. Here I am riding Clinker round Stringybark Mill and I'm not even afraid. How ever did it happen?

Queenie called to her from the river.

"Sophie! I'm washing Ma's sheets for her! Come and help when you get off that horse!"

Auntie Dot usually boiled up her sheets in kerosene tins over a fire in the back yard but they were having a cold-water wash today. When Sophie ran down to join Queenie, the sheets were trailing in the river and Queenie was rubbing them vigorously with a block of hard yellow soap and pounding them on the flat stones just under the water. Soapy bubbles ran away downstream. Sophie rubbed and banged beside her till the sheets were clean. Then they twisted them between them into long white ropes till all the water was squeezed out of them.

"Queenie!" said Sophie, rubbing her wet hands on her dress.

"Mmm."

"Today's the day, you know! Have you forgotten?"

"What day?"

"The day Mr Greenbank said we'd get the surprise. I saw him setting off for Forrest very early. All by himself with Diamond pulling one of the timber trucks. I think he's gone to get it."

"It can't be the teacher then. He'd need two of those trucks for the furniture. And for the family. And he'd take another man with him to help load the stuff on board."

"What can it be then?"

"Pa's given up the idea of a saw. He thinks it's going to be a piano. For the billiard shed. For the sing-songs."

"But who could play it?"

"Ma can. And so can Mrs Greenbank. We could have singing in the shed every Saturday, just like Christmas."

"I hope he brings the letters anyway. There was nothing from Mother last week. She's never missed a week before. I hope she's all right."

"That Mrs Dunphy said she was all right—apart from being as big as a barn." Queenie giggled but Sophie frowned.

The mill whistle boomed out for the midday break. The steam saw stopped at once and fifteen minutes later the logging crew trudged in from the bush with their string of horses. Sophie helped Queenie and Auntie Dot to peg out the clean wet sheets on a long line that ran from the back door to the lavatory right up in the far corner of the yard. Lottie and Effie came back with a netful of blackfish they'd caught by themselves at a deep pool half a mile upstream. Uncle Ted left his anvil and Grandpa walked up from the stables where Clinker was resting. The whole family sat down at the table for dinner. Stringybark Mill was always quiet and peaceful at this time of day. Even the dogs were silent, gnawing contentedly at their bones outside every back door.

"Listen!" said Sophie, a forkful of Irish stew half way to her mouth. She had turned her head towards the window.

"What is it?" asked Queenie, looking up.

"Listen! I can hear something!"

Everyone stopped eating and listened. A faint and regular pounding noise came from somewhere far away in the bush. Nearer and nearer. Louder and louder.

"It's the saw at the mill starting up early!" said Auntie Dot crossly. "And we've hardly sat down! That's not right!"

"No, Dot. It's not the saw," said Uncle Ted, standing up abruptly. "It's not coming from the mill at all. It's somewhere way down beyond the tunnel. Let's go outside and have a look."

They left their dinner cooling on the table and rushed to the verandah. Every other verandah in the little township was crowded. Every family leant over the rail, listening intently to the strange mysterious throbbing that was shattering the midday stillness of the bush. Now they could hear a hissing above the pounding. Nearer and nearer. Breathing and hissing. Bertie began to cry. He clung to Auntie Dot and buried his face in her shoulder.

"There it is!" shouted Uncle Ted in amazement, pointing down to the spot where the tramway from Forrest ran out of the trees. "It's a loco, Dot! Look, me darling, look!"

And sure enough a low squat steam engine with white smoke belching from its chimney in spurts was chugging steadily along the rails towards the mill. The boiler gleamed with fresh black paint.

A sharp high-pitched whistle ripped through the air. There in the driver's cabin behind the boiler stood Mr Greenbank himself, waving excitedly to his people on the packed verandahs as the little engine steamed closer. And Mr Greenbank was not alone. On one side of him, leaning out of the cabin and smiling triumphantly, was Mr Hooker! On the other side and half hidden from sight was Norm Drake! Norm Drake was driving the loco! He glanced carefully ahead of him along the track to measure the distance to the mill with a practised eye.

With a sudden rush of steam and another ear-splitting whistle, the loco pulled up at the landing platform. Inside the stables a horse neighed loudly in fright.

Bertie looked up from Auntie Dot's shoulder.

"Puff-puff!" he cried happily and slithered out of her arms to run full-tilt down the pathway to the mill. Everyone seemed to be running with him. Every verandah was suddenly empty. Fallers and loggers, blacksmith and horseman, women and children—all raced together to see the engine. The dogs left their bones and ran too, barking and yapping. Sophie ran with Queenie. Only Grandpa stood rooted to the spot, his veined hands clutching the verandah rail, his old eyes staring down unbelievingly at the strange black loco by the mill. He shook his head slowly from side to side.

Mr Greenbank had leapt down from the driver's cabin.

"Here we are!" he called to the crowd. "A loco for Stringybark Mill! Now we're as good as any of them!"

He patted the hot breathing monster proudly and ran his fingers over the silver letters of its name on the side. "SERPENT".

"It's costing me a pretty packet but worth every penny of it, eh, Hooker?"

Mr Hooker nodded and beamed, wiping his forehead with a large red handkerchief and jumping down from the cabin with the blue bag. Norm Drake with black oily hands and an old greasy rag was busy polishing up all his knobs and levers at the controls. He looked quite at home now. The anxious look had gone. He alone was in charge of this thing and only he understood its mysteries. He even seemed to Sophie to have grown an inch taller since Sports Day but she knew that wasn't very likely.

The crowd surged up to the engine and swarmed all over it in excitement.

"A loco for Stringybark Mill!" repeated Mr Greenbank. "That's just what we've been needing all these years. Now we'll double our output in no time. We'll never look back. The good times are coming all right. The good times are coming!"

"But, Mr Greenbank," said Uncle Ted who stood puzzled by the loco, running his hands through his hair, "what about the horses? Won't we need our horses any more?"

"Horses? Of course we'll need them, Ted. This loco can't do everything, you know. It's fine on the rails but it can't drive down into the gullies where the horses go to lug the big logs up. Naturally, we mightn't need so *many* horses. We might have to let a few of the old ones go. They've earned a good rest now, haven't they? This loco's going to change our lives, Ted. Doesn't need food—only coal and water. Never gets tired. Never gets sick. Hauls twice the load of all our horses strung together. Yes, the good times are coming all right. Don't you worry about the horses, Ted. Now back to your dinners, everyone. The rest of the day's a holiday! Free rides this afternoon—out into the bush past Coldwater Creek and back again." He turned to Mr Hooker. "Come on up to the house, Hooker, and bring your mate along too. The wife'll have something special in the pot up there! What a day it is for Stringybark Mill!"

Mr Greenbank led the two men up the hill. Slowly the crowd dispersed. The shining black steam engine stood silent and deserted by the mill. Uncle Ted was thoughtful as he reached the verandah with Sophie and Queenie beside him and the rest of the family just behind. Grandpa was still standing in the very place where they'd left him.

"The boss reckons the good times are coming," Uncle Ted said to him a little uncertainly.

"You mark my words, Ted," said Grandpa, still gazing down at the loco. "It's the end of the horses."

"No, no, Dad!" said Auntie Dot cheerfully. "Come on inside and eat up. Mr Greenbank says we'll still need the horses. Or most of them, anyway. Only the old ones might have to go."

"Is Clinker very old?" Sophie's voice squeaked with sudden fear.

"Pretty old, dear," said Auntie Dot. "Needs a good rest, Mr Greenbank says. Now do sit up everyone and eat this blessed meal. If it's not all ruined, that is."

The Irish stew was cold. No one had much appetite for it now but Auntie Dot insisted. Only Bertie was blissfully happy, pushing bits of brown bread around in the gravy and saying over and over again to himself,

"Puff-puff, puff-puff, puff-puff!"

"And who's going to drive the darned thing?" asked Uncle Ted when the meal was over. "I hope that Drake bloke's not going to stay. He'd never fit in at the mill. But there's not one single engine driver in this place. We're all horsemen down here."

"Maybe Mr Greenbank'll drive it himself," suggested Queenie. "He does seem very keen on it."

"I doubt it, me darling. He likes to be at the mill all day keeping a good eye on the saw. He won't want to be right out in the bush hauling logs."

"Well, Mr Drake'll just have to show someone how to drive it, won't he?" said Auntie Dot briskly as she cleared away the pudding dishes.

"It's not going to be *me*, me darling! That's one thing you can be sure of! I'm sticking to blacksmithing, come what may!"

"But, Uncle Ted," said Sophie, "when there's no horses, the mill won't need a blacksmith."

"There'll always be horses here, me darling, and they'll always need a blacksmith! This loco business is just a passing craze. It'll come and go again. Just a craze. But those big horses! They're a different matter altogether. You can't have a sawmill without horses!"

Uncle Ted sounded cheerful enough but Sophie saw how his eyes kept glancing anxiously across to Grandpa who sat silent in his chair, shaking his white head sadly from time to time. Grandpa seemed suddenly much older.

"You mark my words, young Ted," he said again. "That damned loco'll be the end of our horses!"

Free rides for everyone! And the whole mill closed down for the rest of the day! Sophie could hardly wait for it all to begin. She pushed right out of her mind the worrying thoughts about Clinker and hurried to the landing platform with the rest of the family. Only Grandpa stayed at home again. He wanted a snooze, he said. A snooze in peace and quiet.

Everyone was there already, crowded round the steaming loco. Three timber trucks had been coupled on to the engine, one behind the other with planks across each one to sit on. Norm Drake was grinning from the driver's cabin and Mr Hooker stood beside him, his big coat gone and his sleeves rolled up.

"All aboard!" called Mr Greenbank. "Kiddies on first, then everyone else. There's plenty of room. We'll come back for more if you can't fit on this time."

Sophie and Queenie scrambled up on to the front truck with Bertie between them. Lottie and Effie sat close behind. The mothers climbed up onto the second truck, the fathers onto the third. Everyone was jammed close together, side by side and back to back with legs hanging down on every outside edge. Somehow there was just room for everyone.

Mr Greenbank walked along from the engine to the men's truck.

"We're going to need a driver at the mill," he called up to them. "Norm Drake's only here for a day or two. Someone'll have to learn the job and we might as well start right now. Who wants the job? Any volunteers?"

There was an excited shout from all the little boys on the first truck. They all wanted the job. Queenie shouted too. But the men were strangely silent. No one spoke. Then one lone voice came from the crowd packed onto the men's truck.

"Yes, Mr Greenbank! I'd like the job!"

Queenie gasped. She grabbed Sophie's arm.

It was Ron! Ron Vickers! Uncle Ted's mate at the forge. The second blacksmith.

Ron had already jumped down from the truck and was bounding along to the loco. His dark eyes were shining with excitement.

"But Ron!" protested Uncle Ted indignantly, raising his voice. "You can't do that! I need you at the forge! Let someone else have the driver's job!"

Ron looked embarrassed. He paused with one foot already up in the driver's cabin and the other still on solid ground.

"There's not going to be so much work at the forge now, Ted," he mumbled. "We've got to move with the times, you know. Blacksmithing's on the way out. I can't miss a chance like this." And he pulled himself up into the cabin to stand next to Norm Drake under the black metal canopy. Norm Drake guided Ron's hand to the whistle cord. He jerked it once, twice, and the whistle shrieked. Again the horses in the stable whinnied in fright and shifted their feet. A loose board in one of the stalls was kicked to splinters.

"We're off!" shouted Mr Greenbank as he joined the cheering children on the first bogie. The steam hissed. The engine began its steady, breathing huffing and puffing. The pistons moved smoothly backwards and forwards. The iron wheels turned and the little train rolled slowly away from the mill and out into the bush towards Coldwater Creek. Everyone was on board—everyone except Grandpa. And everyone was singing—everyone except Uncle Ted who sat puzzled and silent, thinking about Ron. Up in the cabin, Ron himself was blissfully happy driving the loco under Norm Drake's watchful eye.

A young wallaby grazing down the tram-track hopped away in alarm as the engine gathered speed and roared along the rails. Sophie watched him bounding between the trees, his strong tail and back legs propelling him forward with every leap. Another blast on the whistle sent a flock of pink galahs screeching overhead.

At the first bridge the singing on board suddenly stopped as the loco snorted and grumbled its way high above the water in the gully below. The tall struts underneath seemed to Sophie to sway a little but the bridge held firm under the great weight of iron. The loco pulled the trucks effortlessly to the far side of the gully and through the short tunnel. Faster and faster moved the pistons and faster turned the wheels, clicking and clanking over the rails. Mr Hooker shovelled in more coal and the steam hissed. Coldwater Creek flashed by on the right. The second bridge rattled underneath them. The crowd was singing again by now, happy and excited. At the far end of the tram-track the loco slowed and stopped, still puffing contentedly. Norm Drake showed Ron how to move his levers to put the engine into reverse. Slowly at first, the whole procession began to move backwards, pushed not pulled by the loco. They gathered speed again and thundered along at a fine spanking pace with the steaming engine behind them, over the bridges, up the rises, along beside the river and back through the bush to the quiet mill.

At the landing platform the mothers and fathers climbed stiffly down from the trucks, somewhat relieved to be safely home again. But the children refused to get off.

"More! More!" they shouted. "Please, Mr Greenbank! Just once more to the end of the track!"

"Just once more then," said Mr Greenbank, smiling from his seat in the middle of all the children. "But we need to have your Grandpa with us this time, Queenie. Run up and get him while they're stoking the engine. Harry Daniels is the oldest man on this mill. We must have him on board today."

Queenie ran up the slope to the blacksmith's shop and bounded up the steps of the house.

"Grandpa!" she called. "Mr Greenbank wants you to come for ride on the new loco. Come on! It's quite safe."

"I daresay it's safe enough, lass. I'm not worried about that," said Grandpa. He didn't move from his chair. "But I just hate the thing! All that noise, scaring my horses. All that smoke and soot. It's not natural!" Grandpa folded his hands together on his lap. "You go on and enjoy yourself, Queenie, but don't expect me to join in the fun. I'm too old for all that new-fangled nonsense."

Queenie pulled on his hands.

"Please, Grandpa! Only one ride. With all the kids. Mr Greenbank specially asked you to come."

"Bill Greenbank's got no sense!" grumbled Grandpa, but he did slowly push himself to his feet. With one hand on Queenie's shoulder and one on his stick, he hobbled down to the mill.

"Good on you, Harry!" called Mr Greenbank. "Hop up in front there and ride with the driver. They can squeeze you in somehow. You get the best view in the world up there. I'll stay on here with the youngsters."

Grandpa hoisted himself up into the driver's cabin and stood beside Ron with Mr Hooker and Norm Drake behind him. There wasn't much room and Grandpa certainly didn't look very happy. Back on the first truck, Mr Greenbank took Bertie onto his knee.

"Blow me down, Sophie!" he said with a start. "I've just remembered your letter! It's here in my pocket. And another for your Grandpa. Picked them up in the Post Office in Forrest this morning. All this excitement over the steam engine made me forget about them. Here you are. You'd better take them both. Hold them tight now!"

Sophie looked at the letters. One for her and one for Grandpa. Both in her mother's handwriting. Why was she getting a letter all to herself instead of the usual page in with Grandpa's? Was it good news or bad? She was about to tear her own letter open when the whistle blew and the loco shuddered, steamed, jerked and pulled away steadily into the bush again. The letter would have to wait. She tried to catch Grandpa's attention when he glanced back at the children's truck. She waved the two letters in her hand.

"Letters from Mother!" she shouted up to him against the pounding of the engine and the white gritty smoke that blew into her eyes. But he couldn't possibly hear her. She pushed the two letters safely into her pocket and swayed from side to side with all the others as the little train rounded a bend in the track. The singing started up again with Mr Greenbank taking the lead.

The puffing steam engine reached the first bridge much sooner than Sophie had expected. She was still used to the slow plod of horses or the even slower plod of her own two feet. The green gully opening up below her was thick with the tall drooping tree-ferns. She could just catch a glimpse of the little river itself, still full to the brim but no longer quite overflowing its banks. The water tumbled and swirled between rocks and stones.

They were half way across the bridge. The black loco puffed confidently; the rails beneath the wheels clanked and rang with a hollow echo. A sudden loud crack, like a giant gun going off in their ears, exploded somewhere down under their dangling feet. The bridge seemed to sway on its long slender pillars of wood. Another crack, louder and longer than the first! Sophie shrieked and clung hard to Mr Greenbank's arm. The bridge had snapped! Just ahead of them, slowly and terribly, the loco was tipping forwards, toppling headlong down to the creek. A gaping black hole full of broken timbers yawned in front of them. Now all the children were screaming in terror as they were dragged towards the hole.

"Jump, kids, jump!" yelled Mr Greenbank and with Bertie still in his arms he leapt from the rolling truck onto the planks of the swaying bridge. By some instinct to save their lives before it was too late, every child leapt with him, some to the right of the bogie and some to the left. They fell heavily onto the narrow space between the track and the edge, twisting their ankles and cutting the skin on their knees. Splinters pushed into the palms of their hands. The truck rolled on without them and hung precariously over the great gap in the bridge, its wheels caught and held in the ugly mesh of broken wooden girders.

A sharp pain wrenched Sophie's arm. She scrambled desperately to her feet, sobbing and crying, and hurtled with all the others back across the tottering remains of the bridge to the solid land again. Mr Greenbank stood there, his face white with shock, terrified children screaming all around him and clutching at his legs and arms. He gazed down unbelievingly into the gully below. Sophie ran to the very edge, lay down flat on the bracken and looked over. Far down amongst the green tree-ferns by the brink of the river, the black loco lay on its side, steam hissing and spurting angrily, pistons still moving slowly and wheels still turning in the air. Norm Drake sat dazed by the engine, the blue bag clutched on his knees. Ron was climbing out of the cabin with blood pouring from his head. No sign at all of Mr Hooker. And there, with his white hair trailing in the water, lay Grandpa, his legs and arms spread wide apart, his stick still grasped in his hand.

"Grandpa!" shrieked Sophie.

Mr Greenbank shook himself free from the crying children and was over the edge of the gully in an instant, slipping, falling, scrambling to the bottom. He bent over the motionless figure of Grandpa, touching his face, his hands, his heart. Sophie watched, her eyes stinging and burning, as Mr Greenbank stood up again, stiffly and awkwardly as if his back hurt him. Sadly he shook his head. He took off his coat. He bent down again and heaved Grandpa bodily away from the water. He laid him gently on the moss and maidenhair fern and covered his face with his coat. As he climbed heavily up the side of the gully again with Norm Drake and Ron staggering and limping beside him, tears were pouring down Mr Greenbank's face. Sophie could not bear to look. She turned back to the mob of children, huddled together on the tram-track, silent now with shock.

"Queenie! Queenie!" she called and ran sobbing towards her. "Grandpa's dead!"

11. *Clinker*

With one arm around Ron's shoulders, holding him up as he lurched beside him, Mr Greenbank led the crowd of shivering children back along the tramline to Stringybark Mill. Norm Drake trailed a few yards behind them all, his bag still in his arms.

The mill looked uncannily quiet and peaceful. Hardly anyone was in sight — only one or two men contentedly digging over the damp black earth in their gardens. Mr Greenbank stood still at the edge of the bush and shouted up to the grey houses on the hillside.

"Accident! Accident! The bridge is down at Deep Gully!"

The digging men jerked their heads up at once. They dropped their spades and ran down towards the children. Every door flew open. The little paths were suddenly full of mothers and fathers, running, running.

"What is it?"

"Where's the loco?"

"What's happened?"

"Look at Ron! Look at that blood!"

"Take him home, someone! He needs a doctor!"

"Where's my kid?"

"Get the horses!"

"Where's old Harry?"

"Yes, where's old Harry Daniels?"

"Queenie! Sophie! Where's Grandpa?"

This last cry was Auntie Dot, calling out with fear in her voice as she snatched up Bertie into her arms and hugged him close. Uncle Ted was just behind her, reaching out for Lottie and Effie and grabbing onto Queenie and Sophie all at the same time.

"Where's Grandpa?" Uncle Ted repeated Auntie Dot's question and Auntie asked it again and again, angrily now.

Queenie couldn't speak. She buried her face in Uncle Ted's shirt. It was Sophie who had to answer. Slowly she stuttered out the terrible, unbelievable words.

"He's dead, Auntie! He's dead! He's lying at the bottom of

the gully with a black coat over his face!"

Auntie Dot began to cry, not loudly but with great silent heaving sobs that choked in her throat.

"Dead!" she gasped. "He said that blasted loco would mean the end of his horses! And now it's the end of him!"

"We're not having that damned thing at this mill!" shouted Uncle Ted. "Get rid of it, Mr Greenbank! And get rid of it quick or we'll all be leaving!"

A growl of angry agreement went up from the crowd that had gathered close around Mr Greenbank and the children.

"I'm sorry, Ted," said Mr Greenbank quietly. "I'm really sorry. He was a great man with the horses, Harry was. And he didn't want the loco. You're right there. But we can't turn the clock back. Every mill needs a loco these days. We'll just have to drag it up out of the gully and get it mended. And we'll have to build the bridge again. Stronger this time. Much stronger."

"And how do you think you're going to get it up again?" roared Uncle Ted, standing close to Mr Greenbank and bellowing right into his face. "It weighs a ton! It weighs ten tons! I don't know what it weighs! The job's impossible. Leave the thing down there in the gully till it rusts away. We never want to see it again!"

"The horses, Ted. The horses," said Mr Greenbank patiently. "They can pull the loco up out of the gully. There's nothing those big horses can't do. But Ted, let's forget about the loco just now. We've got to get Ron here to the doctor in Forrest. And we need to get poor old Harry's body up out of the gully. And we've got to look for that bloke Hooker. I couldn't see a sign of him anywhere."

"Damn the man!" bawled Uncle Ted, his face flaming as red as his hair and beard. "He brought that bloody loco here! If he's still alive, I'll finish him off with me own two hands!"

"Ted! Ted! Come on up to the house and we'll get these poor children to bed," said Auntie Dot, pulling him gently away from Mr Greenbank. Gradually the crowd broke up. The parents and children dragged up the hill to the houses with slow and heavy steps. No one spoke. Mr Greenbank was left standing there on his own. Even Ron had disappeared.

"Do I have to go for Harry on my own then?" he called

after them. His words fell heavily into the silence.

Uncle Ted turned back at once and Ray Sanders the horseman and four of the older men. They didn't want to see what they knew they would see in that gully but they couldn't leave Harry Daniels lying there a minute longer. Ray brought out Bella and Diamond from the stables and harnessed them up to an empty timber truck. The men brought coils of rope and a home-made stretcher. Silently they climbed on board. Ray clicked his tongue at the horses. Bella lifted her head. She seemed puzzled, as if she could sense that something was wrong. She whinnied and began to trot briskly forwards into the bush towards Deep Gully with Diamond's great feathery feet stepping firmly behind her.

Back at the house by the blacksmith's shop, Auntie Dot was putting all five numbed children to bed with stone hot-water bottles at their feet and warm milk to drink. Sophie lay down and clung tightly to Queenie. Then suddenly, just as her eyes were closing, she remembered her mother's letter. She sprang out of bed again and felt in the pocket of her dress. Both the letters were still safely there. She took out her own and carried it closer to the window where the light was brightest.

My dear Sophie, she read in her mother's spidery hand,

I have good news to tell you at last. The baby is safely born and I am over the worst already though I'll be in bed for a few weeks yet. It's a boy and I'm calling him Harry—for Grandpa. I know how happy he will be and I'll write him a letter to tell him when I've finished my letter to you.

Your father is pleased with the baby. He's always wanted a boy so now I hope he'll be satisfied and want no more. Little Harry is so beautiful with eyes and hair just like yours when you were a baby.

Come home soon, Sophie. I really need you now. Mrs Flack is staying on to give me a hand for a while but it's you that I need. You know the way I like things done.

Give my love to Auntie Dot. I hope you've been a good girl and no trouble to her all this time. I'm asking Grandpa to come and see the baby. Perhaps he'll come back with you. Your father never likes the bother of visitors as you know but he says that Grandpa can come this once.

Mrs Dunphy's been out to see me and to bring my shopping. She drove out in her buggy with that old horse of hers between the shafts. She's a true friend. She gave me a good report of you at the Sports Day in Forrest.

Come soon, Sophie. As soon as it's convenient for your Uncle Ted to bring you to Forrest and put you on the train. Let me know when you're coming and I'll ask your father to meet you at the station.

With very much love from

Your Mother

Sophie crept to the kitchen but it was empty. Auntie Dot must have gone down to the mill to wait for Uncle Ted and the other men to come back from the gully. She put the letter, spread open, on the kitchen table for Auntie Dot to see when she came in. She ran back to the bedroom, climbed in beside Queenie, pulled the grey blanket up over her head and cried herself to sleep.

The next day was so warm and sunny, the sky so blue, the trees around the mill so green, that Sophie simply couldn't believe that Grandpa wasn't enjoying the new day as he'd always done before. Auntie Dot told her about the men's expedition to Deep Gully. They'd found Mr Hooker in the end. He was pinned right under the loco, alive but unconscious, his left leg hopelessly crushed. They'd had to take Bella and Diamond the long way round to a place where they could easily reach the river and then back up the gully to the fallen bridge. The two horses had heaved on the long chains linked to the loco and managed to shift it a few inches. Just enough to free Mr Hooker's trapped leg. The men had brought him to the top on the stretcher and put him on the bogie. Then they'd gone down again for Grandpa. It had taken Uncle Ted a while to bring the horses down the gully and up to the tramway again. Then they'd brought Grandpa's body and Mr Hooker back along the track to the mill, lying side by side on the timber truck. Two of the men had gone straight on to Forrest with Mr Hooker. They'd stopped at the mill only long enough to pick up Norm Drake. Mr Hooker would've died if they hadn't got him straight to the doctor. Even so, he might still die. No one could tell. He might pull through. Dr Steen would take him to the hospital in Colac.

"I hope he does die!" said Queenie passionately. "He brought that thing down here! He killed Grandpa! The sooner he dies the better!"

"Queenie! Don't talk like that!" said Auntie Dot. She was

calmer this morning. "It wasn't Mr Hooker's fault that the bridge broke. He was only doing his job like anyone else. Selling steam engines. That's his job."

"Pretty funny job!" mumbled Queenie.

"And what's happened to Grandpa? Can't we ever see him again?" asked Sophie.

"Of course you can, dear. We'll all go in together and take our last look at him this afternoon. The men have put him next door in the blacksmith's shop. It seemed the best place. I laid him out myself and your Uncle Ted sat in there with him all night. It's not right to leave a body alone."

"Why not?" asked Effie.

"I don't know why not," said Auntie Dot. "We're just doing what we've always done. It's the custom. And it feels right to me."

Uncle Ted came into the kitchen at that moment, his face tired and dirty, his hair and beard unkempt.

"Mr Greenbank's taken over for a few hours," he said wearily, sitting down at the table. "And some of the blokes down at the mill are making a coffin. Good blackwood they're using. We want the best for Harry. He always loved good wood, didn't he, Dot?"

"Good wood and good horses," she said sadly.

"Will we all wear black, Ma?" asked Lottie with a hint of excitement in her voice. "Lizzie Owens had black when her old Grandma died."

Auntie Dot looked worried for a minute.

"There's no black stuff in the house — apart from my best black dress. I've got ribbon enough for arm bands for you all but that won't do. We should do the thing properly. He was your Grandpa, after all. Arm bands are all right for cousins and aunts but not for a Grandpa. The little store down by the mill is sure to have a good bolt of black stuff. Queenie, you'd better go down straight away and buy me ten yards. I'll run up your dresses this morning and I'll make a little jacket for Bertie. He's got his black trousers and your Pa's got his suit."

Auntie Dot's sewing machine was her pride and joy. She set it up on the kitchen table and her right hand whirled away all morning at the little wheel while her left hand guided the yards of heavy black cotton stuff under the leaping needle. She was a skilful dressmaker and a quick one. By dinner time the whole family was fitted out in mourning black, the girls' sober dresses coming well down towards their ankles.

When the rather scrappy meal was over Auntie Dot took Bertie's hand.

"Now we'll all go in to see Grandpa," she said. "We'll leave your Pa to sleep a bit longer."

She led the five children out of the house, down the steps and along to the forge. Sophie felt odd in black. She'd never worn it before. The new stiff cotton pricked her skin and rubbed roughly at the back of her neck.

The door of the blacksmith's shop was wide open to let the light come in. The fire had been out since yesterday and the forge itself was covered with an old tarpaulin and then a white sheet. Grandpa lay there, dressed in the best black suit that Sophie had never seen him wear when he was alive, not even at Christmas. His eyes were closed and his veined, gnarled hands were folded together on his chest. His face looked smooth and peaceful.

Mr Greenbank sat on a stool beside him. Someone had brought a bunch of wild flowers from the bush and put them on the pillow by Grandpa's head. Sophie could not bear to look for more than a minute. One long glance was enough. She pulled away from Auntie Dot and ran out of the shed and up the hillside to sit by herself in the place she liked best, high above the houses and the silent mill. She watched a line of black ants scurrying back and forth to a heap of reddish earth. They seemed to be in mourning too. She stared at a green rosella preening its brilliant feathers in the sun. Her eyes followed a pair of lizards darting over the bark of a log, their quick tails flicking. She looked right down towards the stables where the horses were being brushed and groomed for Grandpa's funeral, stamping their big feet and tossing their manes. She simply couldn't believe it. Life seemed to be going on all around her but Grandpa was dead. Why hadn't everything else stopped with him? How odd that the breath was still going in and out of her lungs as if nothing had happened. She tried to hold it, one hand clapped over her mouth, but the air rushed out and in again. She couldn't stop it. The world wouldn't stand still for Grandpa's death.

When the horses were ready, coats gleaming, black ribbons in their collars, Ray Sanders lined up all twenty of them one behind the other along the tram-track. Even Clinker was with them now. He stood third from the front after Bella and Diamond.

"There's not much weight to pull," Ray had said to Uncle Ted, "and with nineteen others to do the pulling, old Clinker won't have to strain himself. We can't leave him at home on a day like this."

Three timber-trucks were chained on behind the horses. On the first lay Grandpa's coffin, closed now and heaped with ferns and flowers from the gullies. The men from the mill, all in their black suits and black hats, climbed onto the next two trucks where a row of boxes made more comfortable seats than usual for the journey into Forrest. The women and children stood clustered together on the landing platform to watch the long procession move off with Uncle Ted and Ray Sanders at its head. Auntie Dot and her family were conspicuous in their black clothes, standing in front of all the others.

"Why can't we go too?" Sophie had whispered to Auntie Dot.

"Funerals are just for men," Auntie whispered back. "Women don't go."

Sophie was sorry. She would have liked to have been there to see Grandpa's coffin lowered into the grave. Would the men throw in earth and flowers, she wondered, the way they did in the books she'd read? She stood still on the platform till the last horse and then the last bogie disappeared into the bush.

Auntie Dot's family were not the only ones in mourning. Every woman and every child on the landing platform wore a wide black arm band for Harry Daniels that day. The old horseman of Stringybark Mill had gone.

"How will Mother know?" asked Sophie. "About Grandpa, I mean."

Auntie Dot had taken them all back to the house and made a pot of tea. She cut into the last piece of Christmas cake.

"Your Uncle Ted said he'd send a message by the telegraph. He'll go into the Post Office today when the funeral's over. It's so sad for her. Poor Lily! Just as she was looking forward to showing her little baby to Grandpa!"

"I must get home soon, Auntie Dot. Mother needs me now. I love it here at the mill but . . . "

"You *love* it here, Sophie!" exclaimed Queenie in amazement. "And you didn't want to come! Don't you remember?"

Sophie smiled.

"I remember," she said. "I didn't know what it would be like. I wish I could always live here. With Mother too, of course. And the baby would have to come, I suppose."

"You can't go tomorrow, I'm afraid, Sophie," said Auntie Dot. "It's Sunday. And probably not for a few days after that. Mr Greenbank'll insist on getting that steam engine of his up out of the gully on Monday. It'll take all the horses and every one of the men to do the job. And then your Uncle Ted'll have to mend it and straight away too. If it *can* be mended, that is. I hope it can't!"

"Mr Greenbank'll only buy another loco, Ma, if Pa can't fix this one. We won't be able to stop Mr Greenbank. He wants this mill to be the best in the forest." Queenie explained it all patiently but Auntie Dot wasn't convinced.

"I like the mill just the way it's always been, Queenie," she said firmly, "with the horses just the way they are. Now, Sophie, let's think. It could take your uncle three days to mend the loco. It might take longer but let's say three days. That means he'd be ready to take you home on Friday."

"He needn't go the whole way, Auntie. Just to Forrest will do. I'll be all right on the train by myself and Dad will meet me in Birregurra."

"I rather think Uncle Ted *wants* to go the whole way. It's years since he's seen the farm. And anyway, I wouldn't be surprised if he wanted to have a look at that little Harry of yours."

Sophie felt uncomfortable. Harry wasn't really hers. He belonged to Mother. She didn't want to have too much to do with him. Still, it was nice that Uncle Ted would go the whole way with her to the farm. He'd have to a hire a buggy at Birregurra—or borrow Mrs Dunphy's.

"I'll write and tell Mother, then," she said. "I'll be home on Friday and Dad needn't meet me at all."

The horses did manage to drag the damaged loco along the gully and up to the tram-track and back to the mill. Its wheels still turned so it could roll along the rails. But the shining black boiler was cracked and the chimney had snapped in two. The driver's cabin was badly smashed but there was nothing wrong with the loco that Uncle Ted couldn't put right, given a few days for the job. He didn't want to do it but he had no choice. Mr Greenbank was keeping his loco, come what may, and some of the horses would simply have to go.

But *which* horses? That's what all the men were talking about, out at Deep Gully where they worked hard together on the broken bridge, and in the crowded billiard shed. The women talked about it too. The children talked about it. Everyone had a different list of horses that would surely have to go.

"Bella's getting old, Ma," said Queenie at the tea table.

"But Bonny's got that limp," said Lottie.

"I've never liked Foss much," said Auntie Dot, "there's a mad look in his eye."

"And Clinker'll have to go," said Uncle Ted. "That's definite. I heard Mr Greenbank say it myself."

"But *where* will he go, Uncle Ted?" asked Sophie. "What does 'go' really mean? Will they shoot the horses?"

"No, no, Sophie, me darling. Mr Greenbank'd never do a thing like that. He loves those horses, you know. He'll probably sell them up in Forrest or take them to Colac. They may be getting old but they can still work. Logging's a bit heavy for them now but farm work's not so bad. Even so, one or two of them might have to end up at the knacker's yard, I'm afraid."

"What's the knacker's yard?" asked Sophie, though she had a sudden awful feeling that she knew without being told.

"That's where poor old horses go to end their days," said Uncle Ted and he would say no more though Lottie and Effie badgered him with questions on how and where and why.

"I wish I could buy Clinker myself!" sighed Sophie. "Then I'd take him home. He could easily live in our stables with Dad's two big horses and Daisy. There's plenty of room. And he could work on the farm. Dad's always saying that two's not enough."

"But your Dad hates his horses!" protested Queenie. "You said so yourself. The first day you were here. He'd only hate Clinker too."

"But Clinker'd be *my* horse. I love him. I'd look after him myself. Dad wouldn't care. Just so long as he had no extra bother."

"I'm not so sure about that, Sophie," said Auntie Dot, a worried frown wrinkling her forehead. "Clinker needs a good home if he can't stay here. He's a gentle horse. He's not used to being shouted at—except in a kindly way—and he's never had the whip. Grandpa always coddled him and Ray does the same."

"Anyway, there's no hope of buying him, Sophie, me darling!" said Uncle Ted. "He's getting old, it's true enough, but he'll still cost a good deal more than you've got in your money box. And I can't see your father paying out good pounds for an old horse."

"He'd never pay a penny," admitted Sophie. "And Mother's got no money at all. Only what he gives her for the food. And that's not much. It never lasts out the week."

Auntie Dot looked at Uncle Ted and shook her head sadly. Sophie knew exactly what she was thinking. "Poor Lily!" That's how they always seemed to think of Mother. But Sophie knew they were wrong. Mother wasn't "poor" at all. She was tough.

Sophie wrote off her letter. She'd be home on Friday and Uncle Ted would bring her the whole way to the farm. He had a mate at the pub in Birregurra who was sure to give them a lift. No need for Dad to come and meet them. Sophie knew that that would be good news at the farm.

Mr Greenbank agreed easily to the plan when Uncle Ted asked him. He was so glad to know his precious loco would be back in steam again by Thursday he'd agree to just about anything.

The next day Sophie was astonished to see Norm Drake hanging around the mill again. She hoped he'd gone forever. He'd walked the whole way from Forrest and dumped his bag on Mr Greenbank's verandah. He'd come to see the boss, so Uncle Ted said, but no one could think why. His mate, Jack Hooker, was pulling through in hospital all right but he'd had to lose his leg.

"I'm running the whole business now," said Norm Drake proudly, a new soft brown hat pulled well down over his eyes, as he leaned against the door of the forge to watch Uncle Ted at work on the cracked boiler. Sophie and Queenie were heaving on the bellows to keep the fire good and hot.

"And what *is* your business exactly?" asked Uncle Ted, running a blackened hand through his hair. "Just selling locos? There can't be many people round here who want to buy one of those things. They're not cheap anyway."

Norm Drake laughed.

"We don't just work round here, mate," he said. "We go all over the State. Buying locos. Selling locos. Buying and selling anythink, really."

"Like what?" Uncle Ted sounded suspicious.

"Well, horses for instance. When one of these timber mills buys a loco, nat'rly they need to get rid of a few horses. We can always find a new home for an old draught horse. No trouble at all. Jack's got contacts everywhere. They're all *my* contacts now."

"So *that's* why you're back here, Mr Drake!" exclaimed Queenie. "You're looking for horses!"

Norm Drake nodded and smiled a smile that Sophie didn't quite like.

"No trouble at all, Miss," he said and wandered off down to the stables, his short legs moving fast on the hillside, his new hat fanning at his hot red face.

"I'm going to see Mr Greenbank," said Sophie abruptly. She left the bellows and made for the door.

Uncle Ted stopped hammering.

"Where are you off to, me darling?"

"I want to see the boss. He mustn't sell Clinker to that man!"

Uncle Ted shrugged his shoulders and lifted his hammer again.

"You just stay put, Queenie! I've got to have someone to work the bellows!"

Sophie walked alone to the stables. Mr Greenbank wasn't there but Norm Drake was standing at the door looking in at the empty stalls. She slipped away before he'd seen her and went to try the mill. The high-pitched scream of the steam-saw filled her ears.

"Where's Mr Greenbank?" she bellowed at the first man she saw.

"Up at the house!" the man bellowed back with a smile, waving one arm towards the hill.

Sophie trudged up the path. Her black dress dragged at the backs of her legs and chafed her arms. She undid one button at the neck to loosen the collar. Auntie Dot had said she'd have to wear it for a month but Mother didn't bother with rules like that. Once she was home again she'd wear her old clothes. Mr Greenbank was sitting on the verandah, drinking a glass of beer and sorting through a pile of papers on a low table.

"Hullo there, Sophie lass," he said, looking up at her as she opened the gate. "Going home Friday, I hear. We'll miss you here at Stringybark and that's the truth."

Sophie took a deep breath.

"Mr Greenbank," she said and stopped.

"Mmm. What is it?" He had half an eye on his papers again.

"It's Clinker! Don't sell him! Please don't sell him! Not to that Norm Drake! I don't like his face!"

Mr Greenbank leant back in his chair and roared with laughter. He hit the table with one large flat hand and the paper scattered.

"You don't like his face! Well, neither do I like it much as a matter of fact, Sophie. It's not much of a face. But business is business. If he'll buy my old horses for a good price, I'll sell them, face or no face."

"Sell a few of the others if you have to, Mr Greenbank, but please, not Clinker. Uncle Ted says he might end up in the knacker's yard."

"I don't think so, lass. Clinker's got a few good years' work in him yet. Some farmer'll buy him from Drake. Drake's got contacts. All over the State. He knows where the best markets are these days."

"But, Mr Greenbank," Sophie persisted. "Couldn't *I* buy Clinker? I've got one pound saved up in a box at the farm. I've been saving it up for years. I'd give Clinker a good home. Really I would!"

Mr Greenbank roared with laughter again.

"One pound! I'm sure that seems a fortune to you, lass, but it wouldn't buy much of a horse. It wouldn't even buy you a horse that was lame and blind. It would hardly buy you a bridle. Good horses cost real money, Sophie. Norm Drake drives a hard bargain but I'm expecting a lot more than one pound for Clinker, I can tell you that!"

Sophie turned away and walked down the track between the houses. Norm Drake was coming up as she went down. He looked more sprightly and more self-confident every minute now that he was the boss of the business. She passed him without a word and went back to help Queenie with the bellows. She pushed harder and harder on the handle to stifle the pain and anger that kept welling up inside her. The fire on the forge roared louder and glowed a brighter red.

"Steady on there, Sophie, me darling!" said Uncle Ted. "Don't overdo it. Just let the coals die down a bit. Gently does it now, gently does it."

But Sophie pushed up and down on the huge bellows as hard as ever.

12. *Home Again*

On Tuesday and Wednesday Sophie was up out of bed before even the first whistle had blown at the mill. She ran down to the stables and set to work on Clinker's coat, brushing it down and combing his tail. She helped Ray mix the feed in the manger and led Clinker to the river for his drink. She walked the whole way beside him to the logging site and sat on a stump all morning to watch him work. Her eyes never left him. At dinner-time, Ray gave her a leg up to Clinker's back and she rode him slowly back to the mill, leaning forward against his collar.

"She's getting obsessed with that horse, Ted," muttered Auntie Dot. She spoke quietly but Sophie could hear every word from the verandah. "There's going to be floods of tears when Friday comes. Why can't her father buy her a decent horse of her own. He's got money enough. What the girl needs is a proper riding horse. Not a great big draught horse that's meant for pulling logs out of the bush. She's only obsessed with Clinker because she's never known anything else."

"Mmm," said Uncle Ted. "I'll have a word with Tom when I get to the farm. But I don't think it'll do much good, Dot. He hates horses. Look how he brought the poor girl up to be scared of them. And Lily never rides now. I daresay Tom's scared of them himself. And we know why it is, too, don't we? But Sophie doesn't seem to know a thing about it."

A thing about what, she wondered? When she came into the kitchen she didn't like to ask. Auntie Dot started talking quickly about something else.

On Wednesday evening Sophie was down in the stables again. All the horses had been fed and watered and were back in their stalls for the night. Ray had gone off to the billiard shed and Sophie sat perched on the boards at the side of Clinker's stall. The stable doors were open wide, letting in a little of the light before the sun went down. Uncle Ted was working late. Sophie could hear his hammer still striking the metal of the loco's chimney up in the blacksmith's shop. She liked the half-darkness of the stables and the pleasant smell of horses.

A shadow slipped through the door. She stared. It was Norm Drake. He began to work his way slowly along the line of stalls, peering in a puzzled way at the hindquarters of every horse, taking care not to go too close. He sighed heavily.

"What's up, Mr Drake?" asked Sophie from her high seat by Clinker.

Norm Drake jumped nervously and looked all around him in the gloom.

"Who is it?" he said. "Where are you?"

"It's me. Sophie Ramsdale. I'm up here. Third stall from the door."

He caught sight of her now and came closer. He looked up.

"You know I'm sure I seen you somewhere before, Miss. Not here at the mill. Somewhere else. Ever since I seen you here I keep trying to think where it was."

Sophie waited a minute. Then she told him.

"It was on the train. The train from Birregurra. Before Christmas. You were in the carriage next to mine."

"That's it! The train! You were all on yer own."

"Why did you keep looking out of the window at every station?"

"I was looking for Jack. Jack Hooker. He told me the name of the blasted station but I'd gone and forgotten it. So I had to keep sticking me head out till I spotted him. He was there in the end. What was the place? Dead-end hole it was."

"Yaugher," said Sophie.

"That's it. Yaugher. Funny name."

"And now you're buying up Mr Greenbank's horses," said Sophie, trying to keep her voice calm and to sound as if she didn't care at all.

"That's it, Miss." He glanced quickly up and down the stables and stepped closer still to Clinker's stall. He lowered his voice.

"To tell you the truth, Miss, I'm in a spot of bother over these blasted horses. I'm a loco man, see. Jack's the one that can price a horse, not me. I can pick a good engine all right and I can mend it if it's bust. I can drive it anywhere, rails or no rails. But Jack's the one that does all the talkin', see. And he knows all about horses. I don't know a damned thing. So I'm a bit foxed down here without him. He lies there in his bed moanin' about his leg that's cut off and he tells me to go and get six of old Greenbank's horses. Six of the best, he says. But I can't tell one from another. They all look the same to me. Jack'll go crook if I make a mistake. Maybc you can help me, Miss. You seem to know a thing or two."

"Yes, I can," said Sophie, rather to her own amazement. An idea was just beginning to take shape in her head. She climbed down from her stall and led Norm Drake along the two rows of horses. She took him to the ones that everyone was talking about.

"Here's Bella," she said, pausing in front of one stall. "She's a good horse. A good leader too." She moved on. "And this is Bonny. A real worker, Bonny is. And here's Prince and Foss. They always go together. You could easily sell them as a pair. And then there's Star and down at the end here there's Brownie. That'd made a good six, Mr Drake. I'm sure Mr Hooker'd be pleased with them."

Norm Drake looked relieved. He pulled a grubby envelope from his pocket and a thick stub of pencil. Slowly and carefully he printed the six names, one under the other. BELLA, BONNY, PRINCE, FOSS, STAR, BROWNIE.

He looked hard at his list and scratched his head. He seemed puzzled.

"I thought there was some other one," he said, glancing again along the lines of horses. "Old man Greenbank mentioned some other name. Said he'd have to sell him though he reckoned he didn't want to. Wonderful work-horse, he said. What was the dratted name? Tinker? Blinker? Jinker? Something like that."

"Clinker?" suggested Sophie, her throat tight with fear.

"Clinker! That's it! Which one is he, now? I reckon I'd better just knock off Brownie's name and stick Clinker's in instead."

Sophie walked him back to Clinker's stall, her mind working fast.

"It's a pity about Clinker, Mr Drake," she said seriously.

"Pity? Why?"

"The snake-bite."

"What snake-bite?"

"Didn't Mr Greenbank tell you? Clinker had a terrible bite from a copperhead. A few weeks back. He nearly died but Grandpa nursed him through it. The trouble is, he'll never be the same again. That's what Grandpa said, anyway."

"What do you mean? Never be the same again?"

"It's the poison, you see, Mr Drake. The poison went straight to his brain. That's what's ruined him. He used to be a clever horse but how he's stupid. He can't hear properly either. The poison got to his ears. So he's not much good as a work-horse. I suppose that's why Mr Greenbank wants to get rid of him. You could always sell him as a children's pet—though he's a bit too big for that. He's quite harmless. He wouldn't bite, I'm sure. Or you could always sell him off to the knacker's yard. They'd give you something for him."

"But hasn't he been working on the loggin', same as ever? I seen him goin' out there today."

"Oh yes! He goes out all right. Ray Sanders doesn't like to leave him all alone here in the stables. But he can't pull his weight any more. Ray just takes him along and puts him at the back of the team. He feels sorry for him, really. We all feel sorry for poor old Clinker. That snake-bite's finished him off."

Norm Drake smiled at Sophie. He pushed the paper and pencil into his pocket and rubbed his two hands together.

"I'm real grateful to you, Miss. You've done me a good turn. I might've walked right into a bad bargain. That Greenbank bloke told me a whole pack of lies about this horse. I'll stick to Brownie and Greenbank'll have to find someone else to take Clinker off his hands. Who'd want to buy a horse with a poisoned brain? Yes, you've done me a real good turn, Miss."

Sophie was laughing for happiness inside herself but she kept a serious face.

"Glad to help you, Mr Drake," she said.

"I'll just go up to the forge," he said, "and see how that loco's comin' on. He's a good blacksmith, that red-headed bloke. He's your uncle, is he? Doin' a wonderful job on the boiler. Reckons he'll have it ready tomorrow mornin'. She's a real beauty, that loco, Miss. Just you wait till you see her in steam again. Then you'll see what she can do."

Sophie shivered. The loco had done enough already. Grandpa was dead. But Clinker was almost safe.

"Don't say a word about Clinker to Uncle Ted, Mr Drake. He'd probably tell you a whole pack of lies too. They all want to get rid of Clinker."

"Not a word, Miss," said Norm Drake, still smiling.

When he had gone, Sophie climbed back up onto the fence by Clinker's stall. She told him the whole story.

"I'm sorry, Clinker," she said. "There's nothing wrong with your brain at all. But I had to tell him *something*, didn't I?"

Clinker turned his big head and seemed to nod it vigorously up and down. There was nothing wrong with his brain. That was certain. Sophie skipped back to Auntie Dot's house. Her black dress felt light and airy.

By mid-day on Thursday the boiler was mended and the chimney re-built. The loco was all bolted together again and Norm Drake had her in full steam. Ron climbed into the driver's cabin beside him to take the shining black *Serpent* for her test run down the tramway to Coldwater Creek and back again. Mr Greenbank himself had led the gang of loggers working on the broken bridge. Strengthened with new piers underneath, the old track was relaid across the mended hole. This time it held firm as the loco puffed cautiously across. Mr Greenbank was satisfied. He grinned happily to himself as he walked briskly back to Stringybark. The *Serpent* had come to the mill to stay.

When the loco steamed up to the landing platform after its triumphant run, only Mr Greenbank was there to watch. No one else bothered. They all knew that the loco had come to stay but the accident at Deep Gully was still raw in their memories. It would be years before they forgot.

Mr Greenbank wasn't nearly so pleased when he saw Norm Drake's list of horses that afternoon. Five of them were all right. The very ones he wanted to get rid of. But Brownie? He didn't want to part with Brownie at all. She was still young and vigorous, but Norm Drake wouldn't budge an inch. It was Brownie he wanted.

"Just come along and have another look at Clinker, Drake," said Mr Greenbank persuasively. "That's a fine work-horse for you now! A bargain! An absolute bargain! Not a better animal in the Otways. What on earth have you got against the horse?"

Norm Drake half closed his eyes.

"I'm not sayin' nothink, Mr Greenbank," he said, "but I just don't want that horse. It's Brownie I'm buying, not Clinker. And if I can't have Brownie, I won't take none of 'em!"

Mr Greenbank had to give in. Sophie watched the two men shaking hands over the deal by the stable door. Norm Drake had fetched down his blue bag from the verandah and now he opened it up. He handed over a fat bundle of rather grubby-looking pound notes. Apart from a lot of money, there seemed to be nothing much else in the bag. Only four pairs of very worn shoes.

"You can send them horses into Forrest next week, Mr Greenbank," said Norm Drake. "Wednesdee will do. Jack Hooker's got a mate there. He'll stable 'em for us till we find the buyers. Jack's got contacts, see. All over the State."

Mr Greenbank nodded but said nothing.

Norm Drake strolled along to take one last affectionate look at the *Serpent* in its new shed by the stables and then walked off to Forrest between the rails, his bag somewhat lighter than before.

"Well," said Queenie as the family sat down to Sophie's last tea at the mill. "I hope we never see that man Drake again!"

"I don't expect you will, me darling," said Uncle Ted comfortably. "The boss has got his precious loco now. He's satisfied. He'll never need another. With the fourteen good horses we've got left and that black loco, this mill can run till kingdom come."

"Or till the timber gives out," said Auntie Dot, the old worried crease between her eyes.

"That's a long way off!" said Uncle Ted. "There's always more trees in the Otways. And what beauties they are too! We're darned lucky to live here, Dot, me darling! Trees, trees, trees!"

Auntie Dot nodded and poured more tea.

"It's a funny thing that Mr Drake wouldn't take Clinker, Ted," she said. "I can't understand it, can you?"

"It's a mystery to me," he said. "Clinker's a good horse. Just a bit old for the mill, that's all."

Sophie looked at her plate and the moment passed.

"Eat up, Sophie," said Auntie Dot. "It's your last night with us, I know, but don't be sad. You must come back next summer."

"And every summer!" said Queenie, smiling at her.

"And bring your baby too," said Lottie.

Sophie didn't feel at all sure about bringing the baby. She'd much sooner come alone.

"Anyone at home?" came a voice from the verandah.

"It's the boss!" said Auntie Dot. "Bring him in, Ted, and I'll make more tea."

"Come in! Come in, Mr Greenbank! It's Sophie's last night. She's off to the farm tomorrow. Come and have a cup."

Mr Greenbank came into the room and sat at the table. He looked round at them all.

"It's a sad thing to see you all in black," he said. "Old Harry Daniels'll be missed at the mill for many a day and that's the truth. I can't tell you how sorry I am. I should've made sure the bridge was strong enough. That bloke Hooker said it was but I don't think he knew a lot about bridges. I was wrong to take his word for it. Good old Harry! He always called me Bill and I liked that, you know. Never knew such a man with the horses. Ray Sanders does his best, I'm sure, but he's not a patch on old Harry."

Everyone around the table looked sad and pleased at the same time.

"Thanks, Mr Greenbank," said Uncle Ted. "He was a good horseman, all right. And I can say this. He liked to work for you, Mr Greenbank. Never had a better boss in all his life! That's what he always said."

Now Mr Greenbank looked pleased.

"He was a good father too," said Auntie Dot with tears in her eyes.

"And a good Grandpa!" said Sophie.

Mr Greenbank turned to look at her.

"I reckon you take after him, lass. You've got a good way with those horses yourself and that's the truth. And you're speaking up for yourself firm and strong now too. I'm glad to see it. When you first came to this mill, lass, you could hardly say boo to a goose!"

Everyone laughed, even Sophie.

"So you're off tomorrow, lass?" said Mr Greenbank. "Back to your parents and the new baby at the farm?"

Sophie nodded.

"Met your Dad once. Up in Birregurra. Not so fond of the horses, is he?"

Sophie felt embarrassed. She knew it was true but she didn't like to admit it to the boss. Auntie Dot rescued her by breaking in.

"He had a bad accident with a horse once, Mr Greenbank," she said. "A couple of years before Sophie here was born."

"Did he?" said Sophie in amazement. Mr Greenbank was forgotten.

"Hasn't your poor mother ever told you, me darling?" asked Uncle Ted. "She made a bit of a mistake there, I reckon."

"*We* all know!" said Queenie smugly. "But we promised not to tell."

"Know what?" asked Sophie. She was beginning to feel alarmed.

"About the terrible accident at your farm," said Queenie who could keep the secret no longer. "Your brother got kicked by a big white draught horse. Kicked in the head. And then he died, didn't he, Ma?"

"Sh!" said Auntie Dot sharply.

"But he couldn't have died!" protested Sophie, a panic gripping her stomach. "He was only born last week! Dad wouldn't've let the horses anywhere near him! I'm sure of it."

"Not *that* brother, Sophie," said Auntie Dot gently. She could see now that Queenie had told so much she'd have to tell the rest herself. "Little Harry's safe and sound at the farm. You'll be seeing him tomorrow. But a long time ago you had another brother. Before you were even born. You never ever saw him. Didn't your mother tell you that, dear? It broke her heart when he died. Poor Lily!"

Sophie couldn't believe it.

"What was his name?" she asked suspiciously.

"Tom. After your father."

"How old was he? When he . . . ? When the horse . . . ?"

"Six months."

"It can't be true, Auntie! It can't be true! Mother's never said a word!"

"She should've told you, dear. Now you can see why your poor father's so peculiar about the horses."

Sophie began to cry for the brother she'd never even heard of.

"I wish Dad knew Clinker!" she sobbed. "Then he'd see how good a horse can be. Clinker'd never hurt a baby. He'd never hurt anyone."

"That's true enough, lass," said Mr Greenbank, passing her his large red handkerchief. "He'd never hurt anyone. Quietest horse at the mill. I'm blessed if I can see why that bloke Drake wouldn't buy her. It's a mystery! And Clinker's really getting a bit past this heavy mill work now. Logging's too much of a strain on his heart. What he needs is a good mixed farm. A plough to pull and a harrow. A couple of other horses in the stable for company and a family to love him. That's what he needs."

There was a strange breathless silence around the table.

"Please, Mr Greenbank!" said Sophie at last. "*I* could give him all that! Really I could. Let me take him home to the farm!"

"But your Dad, Sophie!" said Queenie.

"He'll come round. Now Harry's born, everything'll be different. No wonder he's been so hard on the horses," said Sophie.

"And on you all!" said Auntie Dot grimly.

"When he knows Clinker, he'll come round," persisted Sophie, very sure of herself now. "And I'd look after Clinker myself. You wouldn't need to worry at all, Mr Greenbank. Clinker would be safe with me!"

"I believe he would, lass!" said Mr Greenbank. "Take him! And bring him back next summer to see us at Stringybark Mill!"

"Every summer!" shouted Lottie.

Sophie laughed for happiness and, in spite of the sad black clothes, everyone around the table laughed with her.

The next morning Uncle Ted hitched Clinker to a timber truck and Sophie rode with him along the tramway through the bush to Forrest. As she left the mill Mr Greenbank stopped the whining saw for a minute and gave her three long hoots of farewell on the whistle. She smiled to think how that sound had scared her the first time she'd heard it. Auntie Dot, Queenie, Lottie, Effie and little Bertie waved to her from the landing platform. From every grey verandah the mothers and children waved too. The men who worked the steam saw waved from the door of the mill and Mr Greenbank waved with them. Sophie could hardly bear to look back at Stringybark township as the trees swallowed up her slow-moving bogie. She loved it all so much. What a summer it had been! She hung on tight to her bundle of clothes with the sprig of dried box leaves pushed under the rope again. She smoothed her black dress down with one browned hand.

At Forrest station the train for Birregurra was ready and waiting. A cattle-truck was coupled on behind the passenger carriages. Uncle Ted undid Clinker's chains and led him up the ramp and into the cattle-truck. Clinker, didn't seem to mind.

"It's not for long, Clinker, me darling!" Uncle Ted called to the big quiet horse through the window of the truck. We'll be taking you out again at Birregurra and we're not far away."

He helped Sophie into their carriage. The seats were as hard as ever. The whistle blew. The engine snorted. They were off!

Yaugher, Gerangamete, Barwon, Murroon, Pennyroyal, Dean Marsh, Whoorel! At every little station Sophie hopped down and ran back along the train to have a word with Clinker through the window. Then she ran back to Uncle Ted again before the guard blew his whistle and the train moved on. At Birregurra they led Clinker out of the cattle-truck and along the platform to the road.

"It's a good six miles to the farm, Uncle," said Sophie looking up and down the main street. "Who's going to take us? I thought you had a mate with a buggy."

"I have, me darling. But I decided not to trouble him. Clinker here can take us himself. Six miles won't worry him."

"Both of us? On his back?"

"Why not, me darling? He's a working horse. My weight and your little weight are nothing to the logs he's been used to."

"But I've never ridden him so far! I've only walked him round and round the mill. I'll get all stiff and sore. And how will you get back again?"

"Your Dad'll give me a lift tomorrow, I'm sure of it."

Sophie didn't feel so sure. Still, she hurried after Uncle Ted to a tree stump that he wanted to use as a mounting block. In a minute they were both safely on Clinker's back, Sophie in front holding the mane, her bundle wedged between them. Uncle's long legs hung well down but Sophie's stuck out a bit. Clinker's back was so broad.

"We need the reins for this ride," said Uncle Ted, looping them around Sophie and shaking them up and down to tell Clinker to move. "He doesn't know your farm roads the way he knows our timber tracks. Gee up there, Clinker!"

Clinker plodded sedately down the main street and out along the dusty road to the farm. Flies buzzed around them in the dry heat and Clinker switched his heavy tail. As the farm drew nearer and nearer, Sophie's excitement began to drain away. A strange coldness settled on her stomach and she gripped the rough bunches of Clinker's mane more tightly. The whole plan of taking this big horse home with her suddenly seemed crazy.

"Whatever will Dad say?" she asked when the familiar white farm gate came into sight. "About Clinker, I mean?"

"We'll just have to wait and see, me darling. If he won't take the horse, I'll have to ride him back to the mill again, won't I?"

"Oh, don't do that!"

"I only hope your Dad'll have a good drop of beer waiting in the coolgardie when we get there. I'm parched!"

"He won't. He never touches the stuff."

"Pity," said Uncle Ted.

He slid down to open the gate and walked beside the horse for the last mile to the house. There was the oak tree and there was the low box hedge! There was the wide shady verandah and the green vine heavy with leaves and fruit! And there on the verandah was Mother, lying on a long cane sofa, a white pillow under her head! How odd to see her lying down. She was always on the go.

"Mother!" shouted Sophie.

Her mother jerked upright and stared in disbelief at the small black figure on an enormous draught horse under the oak tree.

"Sophie!" she gasped.

Now Sophie caught sight of her father too. He was sitting on a chair further into the shade of the verandah but not far from her mother. He was swaying slightly backwards and forwards, his foot rocking a wooden cradle beside him.

"That must be the baby in there!" whispered Sophie in

amazement. "Look, Uncle Ted! He's rocking it! I never thought he'd ever do that!"

"Neither did I, me darling! It seems to me as if things have been changing a bit here at the farm," said Uncle Ted.

Sophie slithered from Clinker's back down to Uncle Ted's strong arm and then to the ground. She bounded up the path and flung herself into her mother's arms.

"Mother! I'm home!"

Sophie was crying but she didn't know why. Mother fingered the black dress and pulled Sophie down to sit beside her on the sofa. They both looked cautiously at Dad. He had stopped rocking the cradle. He sat completely still in his chair and stared at the greying black horse at the gate.

"Whatever've you got there, Sophie?" he said at last.

Sophie spoke quickly. Her words tumbled out on top of each other.

"That's Clinker, Dad. He's a very good worker. All he needs is a plough to pull and a harrow, Mr Greenbank says. And a couple of horses in the stable to keep him company. And I'd look after him myself, Dad, really I would. And he's very very gentle. He'd never hurt anyone. He'd never hurt a baby, would he, Uncle Ted?"

Sophie paused. Uncle Ted was coming up the path now. He held out his hand to Dad. Dad grasped the hand and stood up.

"Good to see you, Ted," he said.

Sophie was astonished. He'd never been glad to see anyone before. She leant over and peered inside the cradle. The baby had a pink face and a lot of thick black hair. He was fast asleep. She couldn't quite believe he was real and she put out one finger to touch him. His blue eyes opened.

"That Clinker's a darned good horse, Tom," Uncle Ted was saying. "Sophie's right, you know. He'd never hurt anyone. Not if he's treated proper. And your Sophie here's a real good one with the horses. She's got the knack. You can just leave Clinker to her. She can do anything with him."

Now it was Dad's turn to look amazed.

"Sophie!" he exclaimed, looking first at her and then back at the horse.

"And so can I keep him? *Please*, Dad!" she said.

Dad didn't answer. He bent down to the cradle, took out the baby and put him into Sophie's arms. She clutched the bundle tightly.

Dad walked to the front gate with Uncle Ted beside him and looked carefully at Clinker's four feathered feet. He ran his hand down the horse's legs and examined his teeth. He patted him on the neck and stroked the white flash on his nose. He walked slowly back to the verandah.

"Right you are, girl," he said. "You can keep the horse. We could do with an extra one now. We've got to get this farm into tip-top shape for young Harry there. He'll be a farmer himself one day, you know!"

"And so will I, Dad! Just you wait and see! And Queenie's going to be a blacksmith!"

Dad laughed but there was nothing sharp or mocking in his laughter now. He put one hand awkwardly on Sophie's shoulder.

"We'll see, Sophie. We'll see. Let's just put that baby back into his cradle. You sit and talk with your mother for a while. She's missed you. It's been a long time. And since the news about your Grandpa came, she's missed you even more."

Sophie was quite glad to put the baby back. He was so small she was afraid he might break in her arms. She sat down again, closer still to Mother on the sofa. Muffin sprang up and settled comfortably on her lap. Clinker stood quietly in the shade by the gate, one hoof tilted, his brown eyes following Sophie's movements all the time.

"Now, Ted," said Dad. "How about a beer?"

Sophie glanced at her mother in surprise.

"Just the very thing, Tom," said Uncle Ted.

And as he followed Dad into the house he paused by the front door and turned back again to Sophie. He gave her a long slow wink.

Sophie laughed.